Ralph took a step closer. "*Indivisa, etiam in morte*. The Castellucci family motto. It means 'Undivided, even in death.'"

Holding his breath, he pushed back at the memory of his father weeping at his mother's grave.

"And that's why you want to stay married? Because of some stupid medieval family motto."

Juliet's voice was shaking, and he could see the pulse at the base of her neck hammering against the flawless pale skin.

"It's one of the reasons, yes."

She was staring at him incredulously. "Well, it's not enough. It doesn't count. It's not a real reason."

"And that's what you want, is it?" Goaded, he closed the gap between them. "You want something real? I'll give you real."

And lowering his mouth on hers, he kissed her.

He felt her body tense, her hands pressed against his chest, lips parting in protest, but even as he moved to break the kiss, her fingers were curling into his shirt and she was pulling him closer.

Louise Fuller was a tomboy who hated pink and always wanted to be the prince—not the princess! Now she enjoys creating heroines who aren't pretty pushovers but are strong, believable women. Before writing for Harlequin, she studied literature and philosophy at university, then worked as a reporter on her local newspaper. She lives in Royal Tunbridge Wells with her impossibly handsome husband, Patrick, and their six children.

Books by Louise Fuller

Harlequin Presents

Craving His Forbidden Innocent
The Rules of His Baby Bargain
The Man She Should Have Married

Secret Heirs of Billionaires

Kidnapped for the Tycoon's Baby
Demanding His Secret Son
Proof of Their One-Night Passion

Passion in Paradise

Consequences of a Hot Havana Night

The Sicilian Marriage Pact

The Terms of the Sicilian's Marriage

Visit the Author Profile page
at Harlequin.com for more titles.

Louise Fuller

ITALIAN'S SCANDALOUS MARRIAGE PLAN

HARLEQUIN®
PRESENTS®

Recycling programs for this product may not exist in your area.

ISBN-13: 978-1-335-40417-6

Italian's Scandalous Marriage Plan

Copyright © 2021 by Louise Fuller

This edition published by arrangement with Harlequin Books S.A.

For questions and comments about the quality of this book, please contact us at CustomerService@Harlequin.com.

Harlequin Enterprises ULC
22 Adelaide St. West, 40th Floor
Toronto, Ontario M5H 4E3, Canada
www.Harlequin.com

Printed in U.S.A.

ITALIAN'S SCANDALOUS
MARRIAGE PLAN

To my mum X

CHAPTER ONE

STANDING ON TIPTOE, Juliet reached up and shoved her small suitcase into the overhead locker.

It was difficult, though, what with all the other passengers pushing past on their way up the plane. Frowning, she shoved again. But it was catching on something—

'Here. Let me.'

The voice had a definite Italian accent, and it was male—very definitely male. As strong hands made space for her bag she was suddenly aware of the pounding in her heart and the onset of panic.

'There.'

Turning, Juliet felt her panic die and her cheeks grow warm as she gazed up into a pair of eyes the colour of freshly brewed arabica coffee.

'Thank you,' she said quietly.

The man inclined his head and then smiled. 'It was my pleasure. Enjoy the flight. Oh, and let me know if you need a hand getting it down. I'm just back here.' He gestured to several rows behind her seat.

'That's very kind of you.'

Heart still pounding, she slid into her seat. Her skin was tingling. Stupid, *stupid, stupid*, she thought, glancing out of the window at the dull grey runway. Not for thinking it was Ralph but for wishing it was—for letting her romantic dreams of love momentarily overrule cold, hard facts.

Her husband was cheating on her and, aside from the legal paperwork, her marriage was over.

Only, unlike her famous namesake and her Romeo, they hadn't been torn apart by warring families. They had been the ones to destroy their own marriage.

But then they should never have been together in the first place…

Her hands were suddenly shaking and, needing to still them, she leaned forward and pulled out the safety instructions card from the pocket in front of her. She stared down at the cartoonish pictures of a young woman jumping enthusiastically down an inflatable slide.

That was exactly what she had done.

Leapt into an unknown, trusted in fate, stupidly hoping that, despite all the odds stacked against her, everything would be all right. That this time the promises would be kept.

Some hope.

Blood flushed her cheeks for the second time in as many minutes as she thought back over her six-month marriage to Ralph Castellucci.

They had met in Rome, the city of romance, but she hadn't been looking for love. She'd been looking for a cat.

Walking back from the Colosseum, she'd heard it yowling. Just as she'd realised it was stuck down a storm drain it had started to rain—one of those sudden, drenching January downpours that soaked everything in seconds.

Everyone had run for cover.

Except Ralph.

He alone had stopped to help her.

And got scratched for his efforts.

In the time it had taken to walk with him to the hospital and get him a tetanus jab she had found out that his mother was English and his father Italian—Veronese, in fact.

She had also become *innamorata cotta*—love-struck. And it had been like a physical blow.

Wandering the streets of Rome, she'd felt dazed, dizzy, drunk with love and a desire that had made her forget who and what she was.

All it had taken was those few hours for Ralph to become everything to her. Her breath and her heartbeat. She had craved him like a drug. His smile, his laughter, his touch...

They had spent the next three weeks joined at the hip—and at plenty of other places too.

And then Ralph had proposed.

It had been at the hospital that she had first noticed the ring on his little finger, with its embossed crest of a curling *C* and a castle, but it had only been later that she'd discovered what it meant, who his family were—who he was.

The Castelluccis were descended from the Princes

of Verona, and from birth Ralph had lived in a world of instant gratification where his every wish was immediately granted, every desire fulfilled.

Her skin tingled.

And he had desired her.

Whatever else had proved false since, that was undeniable.

Right from that very first moment in Rome the heat between them had been more scorching than Italian summer sunshine.

What she hadn't known then was that wanting her wouldn't stop him from wanting others—that for Ralph Castellucci sexual nirvana wasn't exclusive to the marital bed.

It was just what rich, powerful men had been doing throughout history, all over the world. Taking one woman as their wife, and then another—maybe even a couple more—as their mistress.

Only, idiot that she was, she had been naive and smug and complacent enough to believe that the heat and intensity of their passion would somehow protect her. That they were special.

Remembering the agonising moment when she'd spotted her husband climbing into a car with a beautiful dark-haired woman, she tightened her fingers around the armrest.

It wasn't as if she hadn't been warned.

It was what they did—his set.

She'd heard the gossip at glossy parties, and then there were the portraits dotted around his *palazzo*… pictures of his ancestors' many mistresses.

As an outsider, with no money or connections, she had got the barely concealed message that she was lucky even to be invited through the front door. She certainly didn't get to change the rules.

Rules that had been made perfectly clear to her.

For the Casteluccis, as long as it was kept away from the media and out of the divorce courts, adultery was acceptable and even necessary for a marriage.

Not for her, it wasn't.

Her stomach twisted.

Maybe if Ralph had been willing to have a conversation she might have given him a second chance. But he'd simply refused to discuss it. Worse, after she'd confronted him, he'd still expected her to get dressed up and join him at some charity auction that same evening.

And when she'd refused, he'd gone anyway.

Her body tensed as she remembered the expression on her husband's face as he'd told her not to wait up.

Now there was only one conversation left to have. The one in which she said goodbye.

But first there was the christening to get through.

A shiver ran down her spine.

When Lucia and Luca had asked her to be Raffaelle's godmother she had been so pleased and proud. Unfortunately for her, Ralph was Luca's best friend, so of course they had asked him to be godfather. He would be there in the church and then at the party afterwards, so she was going to have to see him.

There was no way around that, and she had accepted it. But as for the ball...

She breathed out shakily.

The Castellucci Ball might be the highlight of the Veronese social calendar, but a herd of wild horses couldn't drag her there.

She would act the good Castellucci wife for the sake of her friends at the christening, but her cheating husband could go whistle.

Her mouth twisted.

Ralph would never forgive her for not going.

Good. That would make them equal.

The thought should have soothed her, but even now—five devastating weeks after she had fled from the glittering palace in Verona—it hurt to admit that her marriage was over. And with it her dreams of having her own baby.

An air steward had begun running through the pre-flight safety demonstration, and as she fastened her seat belt she curled her fingers into her palms.

More than anything she had wanted a baby. Ralph had too. She'd been planning to come off the pill. Only fate had intervened…

Her father-in-law, Carlo, had been rushed to hospital, and somehow she had simply kept on taking it out of habit.

She hadn't told Ralph—not keeping it from him intentionally…it just hadn't come up. How could it when they never had a conversation?

And later she had been scared to stop taking it.

With Ralph absent so often, and without a job of her own or any real purpose to her days, it had been the one area of her life where she'd still had some control.

And then she had seen him with his mistress, and suddenly it had been too late.

She had been tempted to do what her mother had done. Get pregnant and live with the consequences. But she was one of those consequences and she'd had to live with the aftermath of her mother's unilateral decision. And unhappily married couples, however wealthy, didn't make happy parents…

The flight arrived in Verona on time. It was a beautiful day and, despite her anxiety, Juliet felt her spirits lift. A baby's christening was such a special occasion, and she was determined to enjoy every moment.

She held out her passport to the bored-looking man behind the glass at Immigration.

It would be awkward seeing Ralph, but she was willing to play the wife one last time, for Lucia and Luca's sake.

'Grazie.'

As she headed towards the exit she slipped her passport back into her bag and pulled out a baseball cap and a pair of sunglasses. Cramming her hair under the hat, she slid on the glasses.

She would behave.

And Ralph would do the same.

Her husband might be a philandering liar, but first and foremost he was a Castellucci. And more than anything else his family hated scandal.

There was no way he would make a scene.

'Scusi, Signora Castellucci?'

Her brown eyes widened in confusion as two uniformed officials, both female, neither smiling, stepped in front of her, blocking her path.

Plucking off her sunglasses, she glanced at their badges. Not police…airport security, maybe?

'Yes. I'm Signora Castellucci,' she said quickly.

The younger woman stepped forward. 'Would you mind coming with us, please?'

Her heart started to race. It had been phrased as a question, but she didn't get the feeling that refusing was an option. 'Is there a problem?'

There wasn't.

There couldn't be, because she had done nothing wrong.

But, like most people confronted by someone in uniform, she felt instantly guilty—as though she had knowingly broken hundreds of laws.

'Do you need to see my ticket? I have it on my phone—'

Her cheeks felt as though they were burning. After weeks of speaking nothing but English she knew her Italian was hesitant, and it made her sound nervous… guilty.

The second woman stepped forward. 'If you could just come this way, please, Signora Castellucci.'

Juliet hesitated. Should she demand an explanation first? Only that might slow things down, and really what she wanted to do was get to her hotel and have a shower.

Her shoulders tensed as the first woman turned away and began speaking into a walkie-talkie.

Even though she looked nothing like a Castellucci wife, there was just a chance that somebody would recognise her, and the last thing she wanted right now was to draw attention to herself.

Perhaps she should call Lucia first and ask her to… *What? Hold her hand?*

Lucia was a good friend, and during the first few months of her marriage, when everything had been so strange and scary, she had been a lifeline—at times literally holding her hand.

But she was a big girl now, and Lucia had an actual baby to look after these days.

Besides, she knew her friend. If she called her now, Lucia would insist on coming to the airport. And what would be the point of that? Clearly this couldn't be anything but a mix-up.

'Follow me, please,' the second woman said.

Stomach flip-flopping nervously, Juliet nodded.

They left the arrivals hall and began walking down a series of windowless corridors. People passing glanced at them curiously, and some of her panic returned, but surely it was too gloomy for anyone to recognise her.

'This way, please.'

She walked through a pair of sliding doors, blinking at the sudden rush of daylight.

And then she saw the car.

It was sleek and dark, both anonymous and yet unnervingly familiar—as was Marco, the uniformed chauffeur in the driver's seat.

But it wasn't the car or the driver that made her heart lurch.

It was the tall, dark-haired man standing in the sunlight. Even at a distance, the cut and cloth of his dark suit marked him out. He had his back to her, and she stared at the breadth of his shoulders, her nerves jangling.

No. Not him. Not here. She wasn't ready.

There was no need for her to see his face. She would know him in the darkness, would find him in a crowd with her eyes blindfolded. It was as if she had some invisible sixth sense that reacted to his presence like a swallow following the earth's magnetic fields.

Ralph.

But it made no sense for him to be here.

She had told no one which flight she was catching. Even with Lucia she had kept her travel plans deliberately vague.

Yet here he was. Her husband. Or rather her soon-to-be ex-husband.

She stared at him in silence. Not so long ago she would have run into his arms. Now, though, a voice in her head was urging her to turn and run as fast and as far away from him as she could. But every muscle in her body had turned to stone and instead she watched mutely as the younger official stepped forward.

'Vostro moglie, Signor Castellucci.'

Your wife, Mr Castellucci.

Her breath hitched in her throat and then her hands started to tremble with shock and disbelief.

She was being delivered.

Like a parcel. Or some mislaid luggage.

Her fingers twitched against the handle of her bag as Ralph slowly turned around.

'Grazie.'

His eyes flickered across the Tarmac and he inclined his head, just as if he was dismissing a maid from the tennis-court-sized drawing room of his fifteenth-century *palazzo*.

As she stared at him in silence, she was dimly aware of the two officials retreating. It was five weeks since she had last seen her husband, and in that time she had transformed him into some kind of pantomime villain. Now, though, she was blindsided by the shock of his beauty.

Eyes the colour of raw honeycomb, high cheekbones and the wide curve of his mouth competed in the sunlight for her attention. But it wasn't just about the symmetry and precision of his features. Plenty of actors and models had that. There was something else—something beneath the flawless golden skin that made everyone around him sit up and take notice.

He had a specific kind of self-assurance—an innate, indisputable authority that had been handed down invisibly over hundreds of years through generations of Castelluccis. It came from an assumption that the world had been set up to meet *his* needs. That *his* happiness took precedence over other people's.

Her shoulders tensed. *Even his wife's.*

He was moving towards her and her eyes followed his progress as though pulled by an invisible force of nature. She felt her heartbeat jolt.

She hadn't forgotten the smooth lupine grace with which he moved, but she had underestimated the effect it had on her.

Only why?

Why was she still so vulnerable to him?

Why, after everything he'd done, did this fierce sexual attraction persist?

He stopped in front of her and she felt her breath catch as he tipped her chin up and plucked the cap from her head.

'Surprised to see me?' he said softly.

Mutely, she watched as he lifted his hand in the imperious manner of a Roman emperor, and then the chauffeur was opening the door for her. More out of habit than any conscious intention to obey, she got in.

The door closed and she waited as Ralph crossed behind the car. Then the other door opened, and he slid in beside her.

Moments later, the car began to glide forward.

She felt her stomach muscles clench as he shifted into a more comfortable position.

'Good trip?' he said softly.

His words flicked the tripwire of her nervous anger. He made it sound as though she'd been on holiday, when they both knew she'd run away.

The note she'd left for him when she'd fled Verona five weeks earlier might have been brief and vague.

I need some space...

But the voicemail she'd left him a week ago had been less ambiguous. She'd told him she would be returning to England after the christening and that she wanted a divorce.

Afterwards she had cried herself to sleep, and during the days that followed she'd been awash with misery, panicking about his possible reaction.

But she needn't have bothered.

Ralph clearly didn't believe she was serious.

To him, all this—her leaving, asking for a divorce— was just a storm in an espresso cup that required only a little of the famous Castellucci diplomacy. And so he'd turned up at the airport to meet her, assuming she would back down as every other Castellucci wife in history had done.

Fine, she thought savagely. If that was the way he wanted to play it, so be it. Let him realise she was serious when he got the letter from her solicitor.

Tamping down her anger, she forced herself to meet his gaze. 'Yes, thank you.' She kept her voice cool. 'But you really didn't need to do this. I'm perfectly capable of taking care of myself.'

'Clearly not.'

Her eyes narrowed. 'What's that supposed to mean?'

'It means that, despite knowing the risks, *bella*, you didn't follow the rules.' His gaze was direct and unwavering. 'If I hadn't intervened you would have walked out of the airport unprotected and—'

'And caught a taxi.' She glared at him. 'Like a normal person.'

Something flared in his golden-brown eyes. 'But you're not a normal person. You're a Castellucci and that makes you a target. And being a target means you need protection.'

Her heartbeat accelerated as a flicker of heat coursed over her skin like an electric current. She did need protection, but the man sitting beside her was a far bigger threat to her health and happiness than some random faceless stranger.

He stretched out his legs and the effort it took her not to inch away from him fuelled her resentment. 'If you've finished lecturing me—'

'I haven't,' he said calmly. 'By not following the rules you're not just a target, you're also a liability. You make it harder for the people responsible for your safety to do their job.'

Heat scalded her cheeks and she felt a wave of anger ripple over her skin.

But he was right.

It had been one of the first conversations they'd had when he'd finally told her about his family—how being a Castellucci was a privilege that came with enormous benefits, but that there were some downsides to being an ultra-high net worth individual.

She could still remember him listing them on his fingers. Stalkers, robbery, kidnapping, extortion...

Cheeks cooling, she edged back in her seat. Except the risk today was minimal, given that he'd clearly had her followed the entire time she was in England.

How else would he have known that she was catching this flight?

Her heart bumped behind her ribs.

Besides, if he wanted to talk about rule-breaking, she could name a few he'd broken. Like the vows he'd made at their wedding when he'd promised to be true to her.

'People in glass houses don't get to throw stones, Ralph,' she said crisply.

He held her gaze. 'But I don't live in a glass house or any other kind of house, *bella*. I live in a palace. As do you.'

For a few half-seconds she thought about the beautiful home they had shared for six months. The timeless elegance of the vaulted rooms with their frescoes and sumptuous furnishings, the creeper-clad balconies overlooking the formal gardens and the rest of the *palazzo*'s estate.

And then she blanked her mind.

Did he really think that was all he had to do to get their marriage back on track? Remind her of what she would lose? Didn't he understand that she'd already lost the only thing that mattered to her? His heart.

Battening down her misery, she reached up and slowly twisted her hair into a loose ponytail at the nape of her neck. 'Why are you here, Ralph?' she said quietly.

Honey-coloured eyes locked with hers as his mouth curved at one corner. 'I take care of what belongs to me.'

She looked at him incredulously. How could he say that after what he'd done? He had broken her heart.

But in the grand scheme of things the compensations of being a Castellucci more than made up for a little heartbreak and a bruised ego.

Or that was what everyone kept telling her.

Only none of those things—his wealth, his connections and social status—were what mattered to her. They never would. That was why she had left and why she would be leaving again.

And this time she wouldn't be coming back.

'You have people here. They could have done it for you,' she persisted.

He shrugged. 'I wanted to meet my wife at the airport.' He held her gaze. 'You are still my wife, Giulietta,' he said softly.

Her chin jerked upwards, his words jolting her.

Everyone else called her Letty. He alone called her by her full name, but in the Italian form, and the achingly familiar soft intonation felt like a caress.

The narrowed gaze that accompanied it, on the other hand, felt like sandpaper scraping across her skin.

Her eyes found his. The anger and the bruised ego were there—she could see it simmering beneath the surface.

But that was the problem. He would never show it. He was always so in control.

Glancing across the seat, she felt her pulse skip and her breasts tighten as her body, her blood, responded to the memories stirring beneath her skin.

He was not always in control. Not when they made love.

Then he was like a different man. Every breath, every touch, unrestrained, urgent, unfeigned.

Her breathing slowed as images of his naked body moving against hers crowded into her head. She felt her skin grow warm.

Back in England she had felt so certain, so sure that it was all wrong between them, but being alone with him now was making her second-guess herself.

Only there was nothing to second-guess.

She had seen it with her own eyes.

He was having an affair.

Heart thumping against her ribs, she stared at him mutely, the knot of anger hardening in her stomach. He had deceived and betrayed her, lied to her face. And, judging by the fact that he'd not even attempted to get in touch with her over the last five weeks, he'd clearly been having far too much fun with his dark-haired lover to care about her absence.

The thought of the two of them together made her feel sick, and suddenly she was done with playing games. What was the point of delaying the inevitable? Why not confront him now?

Lifting her chin, she met his gaze head-on. 'Not for much longer.'

There was a long silence.

Glancing up, she saw the glitter in his eyes and it made a shiver run down her spine.

He raised an eyebrow. 'You think?'

A tiny part of her wished she already had the paperwork from her solicitor, so she could throw it into his handsome, arrogant face. The rest of her was too busy trying to ignore the effect his casual question was having on her nerve-ends.

'Did you not get my message?' she asked.

'Ah, yes, your message…'

Slouching backwards, he nodded slowly, as though he was a record producer and she had sent him a particularly uninspiring demo.

'It was all so sudden. I assumed you were being…' He paused, frowning and clicking his fingers for inspiration. 'What's the word? Oh, yes, dramatic. London's theatreland rubbing off on you.'

She held his gaze. 'I want a divorce.'

If she was looking for a reaction she didn't get one.

He merely inclined his head. 'That's not going to happen, *bella.*'

His voice was soft, but there was an unequivocal finality to his words.

'It's not up to you, Ralph.' She was battling with her anger.

He stared at her steadily. 'Now you really *are* being dramatic.'

She wanted to hit him. 'I want a divorce, Ralph. I don't want anything else.'

It wasn't just words. She really didn't want anything from him. It was going to be hard enough getting over her marriage as it was. It would be so much harder if there were reminders of him everywhere.

'I'm not looking for any drama or some cash prize. I just want a divorce.'

His expression hardened, his eyes trapping hers. 'And what are you expecting me to say to that, Giulietta?'

'I'm expecting you to say yes.' Her fingers curled into her palms. 'Look, we both know this isn't working. *We* don't work as a couple.'

Probably because they weren't a couple any more, she thought dully. Now there were three of them in the marriage.

'And that's what you do, is it? When something

doesn't work.' His eyes locked with hers. 'You just discard it.'

She stared at him incredulously, feeling an ache spread through her chest like spilt ink. How could he say that after what he'd done? After what he'd thrown away.

Her eyes blazed. 'Our marriage hasn't meant anything to you for months.'

'And yet you're the one who's walking out,' he said slowly.

She took a breath, trying to control her escalating temper. 'Because you are having an affair!'

Even just saying the words out loud hurt, but his gaze didn't so much as waver.

'So you said. And I denied it.'

Her head was pounding in time with her heart. 'Look, I've made up my mind, so you can stop lying to me now—'

His eyes narrowed almost imperceptibly. 'I didn't lie. I told you I wasn't having an affair. That was true then, and it's still true now. Only you chose, and are still choosing, not to believe me.'

She stared at him, the memory of that terrible argument replaying inside her head. Although usually an argument required the participation of more than one person…

Remembering her angry accusations and his one-word denials, she felt a beat of anger bounce across her skin. 'There was no choice to make, Ralph. I believe what I believe because I saw it with my own eyes.' She drew a deep breath. 'Now, are we done?'

'Not even close.' His jaw tightened. 'You didn't see what you thought you did.'

'Of course I didn't.' She hated the bitterness in her voice, but it was beyond her control. 'So explain it to me, then. What exactly did I see?'

He was silent for so long she thought he wasn't going to answer.

Finally, though, he shrugged. 'She doesn't threaten you—us.'

His reply made her breathing jerk. 'Oh, I get it. You mean it's not serious?' She shook her head, her chest aching with anger and misery. 'And that's supposed to make it all right, is it? I should just put up and shut up.'

'You're twisting my words.'

Her head was hurting now. She was so stupid. For just a moment she'd thought that finally she'd got through to him. But it was all just the same old, same old.

'You know what, Ralph? I'm not doing this with you. Not here, not now.' Leaning forward, she tapped on the glass behind Marco. 'Can you drop me at this address, please?' Glancing down at her phone, she read out a street name. 'It's near the hospital.'

'What do you think you're doing?' His voice had become dangerously soft.

Forcing herself to hold his gaze, she took a deep breath. 'I'm going to my hotel.'

He raised an eyebrow. 'Hotel?'

'Yes, Ralph. It's a place where people stay overnight when they go away.' Watching his eyes narrow, she gave him a small smile. 'I think it's for the best if we keep our distance from one another.'

He stared at her for a long moment. 'You mean you're worried you won't be able to resist me.'

Her skin prickled. 'No, I just don't want you turning up at the christening with a black eye,' she said stiffly. 'But you don't need to worry. I'll play my part at the ceremony, and the party, and I made the hotel reservation in my maiden name.'

Something primitive darkened his expression. 'Show me,' he demanded.

Feeling all fingers and thumbs, she tilted the screen towards him.

'I don't know this hotel.'

Of course he didn't. For Ralph, like all his family and friends, there was only one hotel in Verona. The five-star Due Torri.

She shrugged. 'It's only for one night. I just want somewhere clean and quiet.'

'I'm sure it's both, but…'

He paused and she felt a shiver of apprehension. There was something wrong—a disconnect between his reasonable tone and the glitter in his eyes.

'But what?'

'But if it isn't it won't matter.'

As his gaze drifted lazily over her face a chill began to spread through her bones.

'Because you won't be staying there.'

Her eyes clashed with his. 'Oh, but I will. And there's

nothing you can do about it,' she added hotly as he started to shake his head.

He met her gaze with equanimity. 'It's already done. I've had someone cancel your reservation. It's time to come home, *bella*.'

CHAPTER TWO

WATCHING HIS WIFE'S brown eyes widen with shock, Ralph felt a savage stab of satisfaction. *Good*, he thought coolly. Now she knew what it felt like.

Although there was obviously no comparison between her shock and his…

Gritting his teeth, he replayed the moment when he'd walked into their bedroom and seen the envelope on his bedside table. Even now he could still feel his anger, his disbelief, at returning home and finding his bed empty and his wife gone.

Although, in the scheme of things, that was one of her lesser crimes.

He glanced over at his beautiful, deceitful wife. An oversized linen blazer disguised the curves beneath her dark jeans and white T-shirt, and she was make-up-free aside from the matt nude lipstick she loved.

She looked more like a gap year student than the wife of a billionaire. But, whatever she might say to the contrary, she was still his wife. And that wasn't about to change any time soon. Make that *ever*.

It was five weeks since she had bolted from his life,

leaving no clue about her motives or plans except a two-line note. But he hadn't needed any note to know why she had fled. She'd still been steaming over that row they'd had. A row he knew he could have done more to mitigate.

Except why should he have to mitigate anything?

He had told her the truth. Vittoria was not his mistress. Their relationship was complicated, but completely innocent. As his wife, Giulietta should have believed him. In fact, she shouldn't even have asked the question.

Most women in her position—his cousins' wives and his aunts for example—would have understood that.

But his wife was not most women.

He glanced over at her, watching the flush of anger colour her sculpted cheekbones.

When he'd first noticed Juliet Jones on that chilly afternoon in Rome, it hadn't been for those glorious cheekbones, her bee-stung lips or glossy tortoiseshell hair. In fact, her hair had been hanging down in rat's tails and she hadn't looked that different from the half-drowned cat she'd been trying and failing to rescue.

No woman he knew would have been out in that downpour, much less halfway down a storm drain.

But then Giulietta was not like any other woman he knew.

He had fallen for her beauty and the fire in her eyes—fallen deeper for her smile and her laugh. And then she had made *him* laugh. There had been no doubt, no hesitation in his heart. She was his soulmate. He knew what she was thinking, what she was feeling…

Or he had thought he did.

Remembering the empty packet of contraceptive pills in the bin, he felt his jaw tighten. It didn't make any sense. They'd been trying for a baby—

Except apparently they hadn't.

Hadn't she known how much it meant to him to have a child?

Had he not made it clear how important it was to him to have a son or daughter of his own?

It made no sense, her behaviour. She'd wanted a baby as much as he did—had been eager to start trying. Or so she'd said.

But women—some women anyway—were very good at keeping secrets.

'You had no right!' She practically spat the words at him, her eyes flaring with fury.

'To protect my wife?' He frowned. 'Most husbands would disagree with you.'

She scowled at him. 'Well, it doesn't matter anyway. I'm just going to rebook it.'

With her hair tumbling free of its ponytail and her flushed cheeks she looked the way she had in Rome that first day, when they had kissed their way upstairs to her room.

His stomach muscles tightened. He'd missed her—missed her fire and her spirit—and for a moment he considered running his finger over her soft, flushed curves.

But he still had scars from the last feral cat he'd cornered…

'I thought you might,' he said mildly. 'So I took the precaution of booking all the available rooms.'

Her eyes widened with shock, and then she rallied. 'Then I'll book another hotel.'

'You can try.'

She stared at him, her mouth an O of disbelief. 'You can't have booked out the whole of Verona, Ralph.'

For a moment he thought about toying with her, stringing her along as she had strung him along for months now.

'I didn't need to,' he said finally. 'In all the excitement you appear to have forgotten that the opera festival starts this weekend. You'll be lucky to get a manger in a stable.'

His people had reserved the few remaining rooms that had still been available, but he would have booked every room in the city if it had been necessary. He had the wealth and the power to surmount any obstacle in his path. And when it came to his wife he was prepared to use any and all means at his disposal to get her back where she belonged.

Sighing, he pulled out his phone.

'I suppose you'd better stay with Lucia. I know she has her family and Luca's there. And, of course, she's got Raffaelle's christening to organise, but...'

He watched the emotions chase across her beautiful face, ticking them off inside his head.

Confusion.

Outrage.

Then, last but most satisfying of all, resignation.

'Okay, then.' It was almost a shout.

Snatching the phone from his hand, she threw it onto the seat between them and slid as far from him as physically possible.

'Does that mean you've decided to come home with me after all?'

Momentarily the flicker of fury in her dark eyes reminded him of the flickering candles in the simple trattoria where she had treated him to dinner the night they'd first met.

'I hate you.'

'I'll take that as a yes,' he said softly.

Shifting back against the cool leather, he let his gaze skim over her rigid profile, then down to her tightly closed fists.

She wasn't exaggerating. She really did hate him.

And maybe if they'd been anywhere else in the world he might have been worried. But this was Verona, a city where hate and love were inextricably linked. All he needed to do now was remind his Juliet of that fact.

'Buongiorno, Signor Castellucci. Benvenuto a casa, Signora Castellucci.'

They had arrived at the Palazzo Gioacchino.

Striding into the imposing hallway, Ralph nodded at the small, balding man who was waiting for them.

'Buongiorno, Roberto. Signora Castellucci and I will take coffee on the terrace.'

Giulietta had followed him inside, but now he felt her hesitate. A ripple of irritation snaked over his skin. She had no idea what she had put him through these last few weeks, or how hard it had been to give her the space she'd requested. But he had done it. He'd made himself wait.

Knowing the mistakes his father had made with his mother, how could he not have done?

His hands curled into his palms. He had given her a week, thinking he was doing the right thing, and then two. Two had become four, then five, and then suddenly she was asking him for a divorce.

A divorce.

Listening to her message, all he'd been able to think was, *This cannot be happening. This can't be what she wants.*

Even now it blew his mind—and he knew they would have a short, edifying conversation about it soon. But it would have to wait until after the christening. Luca and Lucia didn't need their special day overshadowed by some bump in his marriage.

And, whatever Giulietta might think to the contrary, that was all this was. A bump.

There would be no divorce. Not now. Not at any point in the future.

'Is there a problem, *bella*?' he said roughly.

She was staring at him as if he'd suddenly grown an extra head. 'You mean other than you forcing me to stay here?'

Anger and frustration clouded her features, and if she'd had a tail it would have been flicking from side to side.

Frowning, he glanced pointedly round the opulent hallway. 'This is your home. I shouldn't need to force you to stay.' He let his gaze rest on her face. 'But if that's how you feel, *mia moglie*, then maybe you need to rethink your priorities.'

Her priorities.

That was the problem.

Surely her priorities should run in tandem with his? She'd certainly led him to think that was the case.

But the empty blister pack he'd found said otherwise…

He heard her take a breath, could see the pulse jumping at the base of her throat as she glared at him.

'You have to be kidding. You know all those beautiful Venetian mirrors in the drawing room? Well, you need to take a good look at yourself in one of them. Because it's not me who needs to rethink their priorities.'

If she'd been angry before, she looked as if she wanted to hit him now. Only why? He'd given her the space she'd demanded. Why couldn't she do the same? Why couldn't she back off and just accept what he'd told her? That what she'd seen didn't threaten their marriage.

But, no, she had to go flouncing back to England.

He shook his head slowly. 'And yet you are the one behaving like a petulant child.'

Her mouth dropped open, but without giving her a chance to reply he spun on his heel and walked away from her.

As he strode through the rooms, past the rare French and Italian tapestries on the walls, he tugged off his jacket and tossed it onto a chair.

'In what way is that true?' She had followed him. 'Tell me.'

They were outside now. She blinked in the sunlight.

'What? I'm being childish because I had the effrontery to get upset that you cancelled my hotel room?'

'Which I did for obvious and understandable reasons.'

Her eyes flared. 'In other words, you were protecting the Castellucci brand.'

His jaw tightened, but he resisted the urge to tell her that as her surname wasn't ever going to change *she* was part of that brand.

'My decision to cancel your booking had nothing to do with my family.' Why was she so determined to think ill of him? 'I was thinking about our friends and how they would feel if their son's christening got turned into a circus by his godparents.'

He took a step towards her.

He had been thinking, too, about his wife.

His chest tightened. It had been hard enough when she had been in London, but knowing she was here in his city, sleeping in some strange bed instead of by his side…he couldn't let that happen.

'I was careful,' she said.

But the colour had drained from her cheeks and he could hear the catch in her voice.

'Not careful enough,' he said quietly.

Even after six months as a Castellucci she still didn't get it. She still hadn't accepted that her life was not like other people's. And, like his mother, apparently she wanted something different—something more.

The thought made his stomach muscles tighten painfully. 'What if the taxi driver had recognised you? Or someone at the hotel? That's all it would take.'

There was a long silence. She was biting her lip.

'I thought it would be awkward…me staying here.'

He studied her face: the full, soft mouth, the dark arch of her eyebrows, the eyes the colour of molten chocolate. Eyes that had lost their anger.

A pulse of heat danced across his skin as the silence lengthened. Did she know how beautiful she was? How much he wanted her? He didn't even need to touch her to get turned on.

But that didn't mean he wasn't interested in touching her.

He was.

He was very interested.

As though reading his thoughts, she lifted her chin and their eyes collided. Around them the air was pulsing in time with his blood surging south.

Reaching out, he touched her cheek, let his hand slide through her hair, feeling the glossy weight. 'Does this feel awkward to you, *bella*?'

Heart pounding, Juliet stared at him, shivers of anticipation tingling across her skin. One second she had been standing in front of him, blinded not just by sunlight but by anger, the next his hand had been caressing her cheek.

Stop this now, she ordered herself, her hands pushing against his chest.

Except they weren't pushing.

Instead, her trembling fingers were splaying out, biting into the cool cotton of his shirt.

And now time had stopped, and everything was fading

into the background, and she was conscious of nothing but the man and the pulsing wayward urges of her body.

Her heartbeat accelerated as she silently answered his question. *No*, this part of their life had never been awkward. Not even that first time—her first time.

Her skin tightened as she remembered those magical hours in Rome.

The tangle of sheets and their bodies blurring over and over again in that stuffy little bedroom.

Before Ralph she'd done things with guys, but always something had stopped her from going all the way. Her nerves, their clumsiness, a lack of the chemistry she assumed would and should be there. But mostly it had been an unspoken need for her first time to matter. Or, more accurately, for *her* to matter.

That was the difference between her and her friends. Obviously they had wanted their first time to be a good experience too, but they'd grown up believing they mattered, so for them it had been more about getting their virginity 'out of the way'.

It had never been in the way of anything she wanted.

Her pulse dipped.

Until she'd met Ralph.

And he had been worth the wait.

From that first caress everything had flowed like water. At some point they had become one, and by then there had been no barriers between them.

Remembering his smooth, sleek skin, and the tormenting pleasure of his touch, she felt her body grow warm. She had known that sex could be quick or slow, tender or passionate, but she hadn't known that it had the power to heal. That it could make you feel whole.

Her eyes fluttered over his body. He had taken off his jacket and he was close enough for her to see the definition of hard muscle and the hint of hair beneath his immaculate handmade shirt.

So close that she could feel the heat of his skin.

Feel the heat racing along her limbs.

But she was over him.

Wasn't that why she had walked out of this glittering palace and away from their life? Why she had told him she wanted a divorce? So she could walk away for ever and move on with her life.

And yet she could feel herself leaning closer, feel her body starting to soften, her pulse to slow. It would be so easy to move nearer, to thread her fingers through his tousled hair, sink into his body and feel that perfect curving mouth against her lips.

There was the clink of china behind her back. For a moment she felt her body sway like a pendulum, and then she took a step backwards, glancing over to where Roberto was putting down a tray on the glass-topped table.

The skin on her palms felt as though it had been burned. Her cheek, on the other hand, felt cool without Ralph's hand there. She took a shaky breath, her pulse ragged with shock and exasperation.

One touch! Was that all it took to make her forget all sense of self-preservation? *Clearly she had been out in the sun too long.*

'Would you like me to pour the coffee, *signor*?'

'No, it's fine, Roberto.' Ralph was shaking his head, but his eyes stayed locked with hers. 'We can manage— can't we, *cara*?'

We.

She felt her stomach flip over. His choice of word was deliberate, and she waited impatiently, nerves jangling, for Roberto to leave the terrace.

'Won't you join me?' he asked.

She turned, her eyes narrowing, as her husband dropped down into a chair and sprawled out against the linen cushions.

'What are you doing?' she said hoarsely.

'I'm sitting down.'

'I meant before. What was that all about?'

He stared at her steadily, his face impassive. 'You said we didn't work as a couple. I was just reminding you that we do.'

She glared at him, the truth of his words only making her angrier with both him and herself. 'We don't.'

'So what was that, then? And please don't tell me it was a mistake,' he said softly.

'It was nothing.'

She wanted to move further away, to get more distance between them, but that would simply suggest that the opposite of what she was saying was true.

'Nothing happened and nothing is going to happen,' she said stiffly.

His golden gaze was direct and unwavering. 'You can't fight it, *bella*. It's stronger than both of us.'

His cool statement made her breathing jerk.

It scared her that he might be right. That years from

now, maybe decades, she would still crave Ralph as she did now. It didn't matter that she would never admit that to him—she couldn't lie to herself.

And what made it worse—*no*, what made it wrong—was that her hunger for him was unchanged even though she knew he'd been unfaithful.

Surely that should have diminished her desire? Eased the ache inside her?

The fact that it hadn't scared her more than anything else. She didn't want to be that woman—to be vulnerable.

Only she was vulnerable where Ralph was concerned.

She knew how easy it would be to give in to the heat of her hunger, to go where he wanted to take her, just as she'd done at the airport.

Her hands tightened into fists.

But it was bad enough that Ralph had betrayed her. She didn't need to betray herself too.

'That doesn't make it right,' she said. 'Just because you want something—*someone*—it doesn't mean it's okay to act on that desire.'

She felt a spasm of pain, remembering the moment when she'd seen Ralph guiding his mistress in the street, the intensity of his gaze, the urgency of his hand on the car door.

Lifting her chin, she locked her eyes with his. 'But obviously I can see why you might find that a difficult concept.'

Watching her face, Ralph felt his shoulders tense. On the contrary, he thought. He'd spent five weeks *not* acting—five long weeks tamping down his anger. Now he could feel it rising to the surface.

He wanted to shake her.

Gazing up at her flushed face and the glossy hair spilling free of its ponytail, he felt his groin harden.

Actually, no. He wanted to kiss her.

Here, now, he wanted to pull her into his arms and cover her soft mouth with his, to strip her naked and make her what she had been before and would be soon enough again.

His.

But he resisted the temptation to act on his desire. There was plenty of time. What mattered was that she was here and not in some shabby hotel on the outskirts of the city.

Everything was going according to plan.

Tomorrow they would arrive at the christening together.

Afterwards they would leave together.

Later in the week she would be by his side like a good wife, welcoming guests to the Castellucci Ball.

And then he would get answers to the questions that had been swirling like storm clouds inside his head.

But for now he would be patient.

Not that his beautiful, baffling wife would believe that was possible...

He stared at her steadily, his mind searching its own corners for words that could douse her fire and fury—temporarily at least.

But why did he need eloquence? Simple and honest might actually work best.

Sighing, he gestured towards the sofa. 'Look, I get that you're angry with me, and we clearly need to talk, but could we just put this particular conversation on hold? For our friends? For Lucia and Luca?'

Her face was stiff with tension, but he could see she was listening.

'It's their son's christening. Our godson's christening. And we might not be in agreement about much right now, but I know neither of us wants to do anything that might impact on Raffaelle's special day.'

There was a beat of silence as her dark eyes searched his face, and then she sat down stiffly on the sofa opposite him. He felt a rush of triumph, and relief.

'Coffee?' he said.

She nodded slowly. 'But, so we're clear. Just because I've agreed to stay here, it doesn't mean I'll be sharing a bed with you.'

Sitting down, he picked up his cup and took a sip of coffee, deliberately letting the silence swell between them.

The Castelluccis had been, and still were, one of the most powerful families in Italy. For that reason alone most women would have burned a path across the earth to share his bed.

Not his wife, though.

His pulse skipped a beat.

It was tempting to haul her across the sofa's feather-filled cushions and demonstrate that a bed wasn't necessary for what he had in mind. But, much as he wanted to do so, what mattered more was that she came to him willingly, wantonly, as she had before.

Remembering the softness of her skin, the urgency of her touch, the smooth dovetailing of her body with his as she melted into him, he felt his groin tighten. And then, blanking his mind, he shrugged.

'That won't be a problem. There are twenty-five bedrooms here, *bella.* I'm sure one of them will meet with your satisfaction.'

Roberto would have had her case taken to their room, but that was easily resolved. The butler had worked for the Castellucci family for thirty years. He was both quietly efficient and discreet when it came to family matters—as were all members of the household staff.

'But you will dine with me tonight?' he said.

He held her gaze…could almost see her brain working through a flow chart of possible outcomes.

Finally, though, she nodded. 'I suppose we both have to eat.' Smoothing down her jeans, she stood up, her eyes dark and defiant. 'I'm going to freshen up. I'll see you at dinner.'

Forty minutes later she was staring at her reflection and wondering why she hadn't just said no.

It was crazy.

She could easily have had a tray sent up to her room.

But, then again, she was going to have to see him at the christening anyway, and it was clear she needed to practise pretending that everything was fine between them.

Blotting her lips, she checked her reflection again.

And she wanted to prove to herself and to Ralph that what had happened out on the terrace had been a one-off. A moment when the past and present had overlapped.

Picturing the up-curve of his mouth and the familiar blunt expression on his face as he'd stared down at her, she felt her breath hitch in her throat.

She knew time couldn't stop or stand still, but just for those few seconds it had felt as though the laws of physics had been disrupted and they were back at the beginning, before everything unravelled.

Her mouth thinned.

And maybe that was a good thing.

Those few seconds had amply proved just how naive she had been, assuming an explosive sexual chemistry like theirs could simply be switched off.

Looking back at the mirror, she adjusted the neckline of her dark blue sleeveless shirt dress.

But, as she'd told Ralph, it wouldn't happen again—whatever she wore tonight needed to reinforce not undermine that message, and this dress was perfect.

For a moment she considered putting a thin cardigan over the top, but that might imply that she needed additional barriers between them.

Plus, it would remind her of Rome…

Her lip curled. *No.* Rome was the past.

If she thought about Rome then it would be all too easy to let good memories persuade her that his betrayal had been a momentary lapse. Particularly now that she was here in Verona…in the home they shared.

Only it wouldn't be her home for much longer.

She swallowed against the lump in her throat. It hurt to let go of the past and the passion. But there was no point in holding it close. In thinking that things would change. That people changed.

Her body tensed.

Been there, done that.

And not just once, she thought, closing her eyes.

For a few half-seconds she let herself go back…let memories float up through the darkness.

Other children had been raised by their parents. She had been forged. So often she had been out of her depth, and always it had felt as if she was waiting and hoping. Waiting for the inevitable. For things to go wrong, for the latest set of promises to be broken. Hoping that this time would be different. Only that had just made the disappointment worse.

She opened her eyes and stared at her pale, set face in the mirror.

Ralph had been right.

Some things were too relentless, too immutable to fight. And, no matter how much she wanted to stay and keep fighting, she knew from experience that the only way to survive mentally, emotionally, was to walk away.

So, however much it hurt, however desperately she wanted to hold on to the dream of her marriage, that was what she was going to do.

Walking downstairs, though, took more courage than she'd thought. Her beautiful home seemed both different and yet familiar, so that she felt as if she was sleepwalking in a dream.

'*Buonasera, Signora Castellucci.*' Roberto greeted her as she walked into the drawing room. 'Signor Castellucci is waiting for you on the terrace.'

'*Grazie*, Roberto.'

She walked outside, her breath tangling in her throat. They hadn't often eaten alone in the evening. He'd worked long hours—longer after Carlo had been taken ill. And on the rare occasions when they hadn't been attending a party or a charity event there had been numerous family commitments.

Her heart twisted.

It was ironic that only a few months ago she'd actually longed for an evening when it would be just the two of them.

She felt her pulse stutter as she spotted Ralph. He was standing with his back to her, as he had at the airport, his gaze directed towards the yellowing lights of Verona. Gone was the dark suit of earlier. Instead he was wearing pale chinos and a dark brown polo shirt that hugged his broad shoulders.

As he turned towards her, she stared at him mutely. The Castelluccis might live in palaces, but they had a horror of the baroque or flamboyant. Ralph's clothes were a masterclass in the kind of high-end stealth-wealth camouflage loved by his family. Inconspicuous, logo-less, but eye-wateringly expensive.

She hadn't realised that in Rome. She'd been too smitten, too dazzled by his beauty and confidence to think about his clothes. He'd told her he was taking a few days off and his jeans and sports jacket had reflected that.

Now, though, she knew that, however casually her husband was dressed, he was rarely off duty or off guard.

She walked towards him, her skin tightening as his gaze drifted slowly over her dress down to her sandaled feet.

'You look beautiful,' he said quietly.

She accepted his compliment. Her plan was to stay cool, but polite, to eat, and then to excuse herself as soon as possible. 'Thank you.'

'What would you like to drink?'

'Sparkling water would be lovely.'

She was careful to avoid his fingers as she took the glass from his outstretched hand.

Glancing across to the table, she felt a flutter of relief. There were candles, but there was still enough daylight to offset any seductive overtones from the fluttering flames.

'Shall we?' Ralph gestured towards the table. 'Unless you—?'

'No, let's eat,' she said quickly.

The sooner this was over the better.

He stood behind her, waiting while she sat down. And, nerves tightening, she held her breath until he was safely seated opposite her.

'So, how was England?' he asked.

She had half thought he might pick up their conversation from where he'd left off earlier, but if he wanted to talk about England that suited her fine.

Ralph's chef, Giancarlo, had run an award-winning *cantina* in Venice, and his food was innovative, quintessentially Italian and delicious. But her stomach was tight with nerves and each mouthful of her ravioli with lobster and saffron was harder to swallow than the last.

'Relax, *bella*. It's just some pasta in a sauce.'

His lazy smile made her chest ache with an unsettling mix of regret and longing.

'But don't tell Giancarlo I said that. He still hasn't forgotten when I asked him to make a Hawaiian pizza for my seventh birthday.'

Her laugh was involuntary. 'Did he make it?'

'Of course. I always get what I want,' he said softly.

Her blood turned to air as he reached over and lightly traced the curve of her mouth.

'You have such a beautiful smile. I'd forgotten just how beautiful, and that's my fault.' His mouth twisted. 'All of this is my fault. I know that. But I want you to know that I can change, and if you give me a chance I will prove that to you.'

The pull of his words was making her breathless. She so wanted to believe him, but—

She batted his hand away. 'I'm sorry, but that's not what I want.'

'And *I'm* sorry, but I don't believe you.' His eyes didn't leave her face. 'Giulietta, we have something special.'

'*Had* something special,' she corrected him.

Or maybe they hadn't. She didn't know any more. That blissful certainty of finding her one true love had been no more than pyrite—fool's gold—and she would be a fool to go back to the pain of loving him again.

'Please, Ralph, there's no purpose to any of this.'

'No purpose to fighting for our marriage?' He frowned. 'We promised to be there for one another, for better and for worse.'

She opened her mouth, then closed it again. She didn't want to think, much less talk about their wedding day, or the vows he had unilaterally broken. What was the point?

'Giulietta—?' he prompted her.

'*What*, Ralph?' Her voice was vibrating with reproach and accusation. 'What do you want me to say?'

His eyes hardened. 'Look, I know this has been a tough time, but all marriages go through rocky patches.'

She knew they did. A lifetime in and out of foster care was proof of that.

But, looking at his face, she felt her heart twist. This wasn't about reconciliation. It was about pride and power. Ralph Castellucci simply didn't understand the word *no*.

She stood up from the table and took a step back 'They do, but not everyone wilfully steers the boat onto the rocks.'

Ralph stared at her in exasperation.

Moments earlier she had smiled a smile he remembered and missed…a smile of such sweetness that he could almost taste it in his mouth.

And, watching her, he had felt a sudden rush of hope that maybe he didn't have to be alone with the truth any more. That maybe he could finally confess to her and then everything would go back to how it used to be.

But how could he tell her the truth? She wouldn't even meet him halfway, even though she was the guilty party. She had lied and deceived him, only apparently all this was his fault.

'It's not me who steered the boat onto the rocks. I can sail with my eyes shut.'

Her eyes narrowed. 'I'm not talking about the *Alighieri.*'

'Neither am I,' he said softly.

She glared at him, her teeth bared. 'What's that supposed to mean?'

It was on the tip of his tongue to tell her. To upend her world as she'd upended his. But he wanted time and privacy for this conversation. Fortunately, he had just the place in mind.

For a moment a strained silence hung between them, and then she took another step backwards. 'I think we're done here, don't you?'

Watching her stalk back into the house, Ralph picked up his glass and downed the contents.

They weren't done. Far from it. But he could afford to let her go. Afford to wait until the time was right. And then he would prove to her just how seriously he took his marriage vows.

CHAPTER THREE

'*EHI*, CASTELLUCCI! OVER HERE!'

Glancing over the heads of the guests gathered outside the beautiful Romanesque church, Juliet felt her lips curve upwards as she spotted a smiling Lucia holding Raffaelle. Beside her, Luca was waving and grinning.

She looked up at Ralph. 'They're over—'

'I can see them.'

Her body tensed as his hand caught hers, but he was already tugging her forward. 'This way.'

How did he do this? she wondered. There was an incredible number of people milling around in the square, and yet the crowd was parting like a Biblical sea as he guided her towards Lucia and Luca.

Following in his footsteps, she had the usual feeling of being both protected and horribly conspicuous—as if every eye was tracking her through the crowd, judging her hair, her clothes, her weight, her suitability as a Castellucci bride.

She had never really got used to it—no more than she had got used to the bodyguards who were an integral part of life for the super-rich. And now, after five peaceful, anonymous weeks back in England, she felt extra naked.

Not a particularly relaxing sensation to have around Ralph, she thought, feeling his gaze and his fingertips on her back.

'*Amico!*'

As Luca grabbed Ralph in one of those complicated one-armed man hugs, Lucia kissed her on both cheeks. 'Letty, you look beautiful. I love that dress.' Her eyes widened. 'And those shoes!'

Glancing down at her dark red heels, Juliet laughed. 'I'm happy to swap. Truly. I nearly broke my neck just walking here from the car.'

Lucia breathed out shakily. 'I'm so glad you're back. Promise me you won't disappear like that again.'

It was a simple exchange between friends, and yet Juliet could feel a tingling warmth creeping down her spine. From somewhere over her shoulder, she was aware of Ralph's gaze boring into the back of her head.

She hesitated, not wanting to lie, but also wanting to reassure her friend. Only the stubborn need to remind her husband that he wasn't calling the shots forbade her from doing so.

'I didn't disappear,' she said quickly, sidestepping the question. 'But I did miss you and…' she glanced down at Raffaelle '…I missed this little one too.'

Reaching out, she gently stroked his cheek, feeling something unravelling inside her as the baby grabbed her fingers with one chubby hand. With his dark, silky hair and huge brown eyes, he was utterly gorgeous.

'Hey, *ometto*…'

Even without hearing his voice, she knew that Ralph was standing beside her. She could feel his eyes picking over her face, looking at her hand in Raffaelle's, and the sharp ache in her heart made her feel faint.

Watching the baby's lips flutter into a smile, Juliet felt her heart contract. She'd wanted a baby so badly. Ralph even more so. Although perhaps it might be more accurate to say that he'd wanted an heir.

A sharp pulse of pain made her press her fingers against her forehead. Was all this her fault? Would it have been different if she'd got pregnant?

Yes. No…

Truthfully, she didn't know. But she did know that if she'd kept on playing by his rules their child would have grown up in Ralph's gilded world. Heir to a fortune, and surrounded by unimaginable luxury and opulence.

Except that wasn't enough.

Not if that world required her son or daughter to grow up as she had—surrounded by lies and compromise and broken promises.

Gazing down at the baby, she felt her throat tighten. She knew how painful that was—knew too that you could never outrun the damage it caused.

Why else had she married a man like Ralph?

A man whose carelessness with people's feelings matched—no, *surpassed* that of her parents.

As a child she'd had no control over her life. She hadn't understood then that her parents' choices had required her to give up something of herself. But she did understand now that if her marriage continued she would be pitched back into the pain and uncertainty of her childhood.

Only she wasn't a child now. She was an adult. And she couldn't—she wouldn't—go there again.

She wouldn't be trapped in a loveless marriage.

Not even for Ralph.

Shifting the baby in her arms, so that Ralph could kiss her, Lucia grimaced. 'He's not so little now. He's actually the biggest baby in our mother and baby group,' she added proudly.

'That's because he takes after his *papà*.' Leaning forward, Luca blew on his son's neck, grinning as the baby squirmed and giggled in delight. 'We Bocchetti men inspire superlatives.'

'Yes, you do.' Ralph grabbed his friend round the shoulders. 'Like dumbest and most uncool.'

Lucia burst out laughing, but Juliet barely registered the joke. It was the lazy smile pulling at Ralph's mouth that had captured her attention and was holding it with gravitational force.

Around her, she felt the women in the crowd crane forward, like flowers turning towards the sun, and despite her resentment she completely understood why.

It was a smile that promised and delivered unimaginable pleasure.

Other promises, though, he found harder to keep.

And yet seeing him with his friends made it hard to remember that.

Her heart began beating a little faster.

She hardly ever saw this side of him—perhaps only

ever with Luca, his childhood friend…the one person he seemed able to relax around.

With his family—particularly the older members—he was serious and formal. And his cousins Nico and Felix were too in awe of his status as heir, too anxious both for his attention and his approval to fully relax with him.

Perhaps he had been different with his mother?

But Francesca Castellucci had died just over a year ago, and although Ralph had told her about his mother's illness he hadn't offered any insights into their relationship.

Her heartbeat accelerated. It was something they had in common, that reluctance to talk about their mothers. Although not, she was sure, for the same reasons.

She had no desire to talk about any of her parents. Not her numerous foster parents and particularly not her biological ones.

Nancy and Johnny had collided when Nancy was just seventeen. Their marriage had been an unhappy mix of easy sex and complicated emotion, and almost exactly nine months from the day they'd met they'd become parents.

Juliet felt a familiar nausea squeeze her stomach.

By then there had already been fault lines in the relationship, and they'd got deeper and wider after her arrival.

For weeks at a time, sometimes months, it would work. But sooner or later it had always fallen apart, and she had always been waiting for that moment to happen, body tense, all five senses on high alert, trying to anticipate every potential flash point.

An empty milk carton.

Money missing from a purse.

A dropped call.

She swallowed. Telling Ralph about her childhood hadn't been an option. She had shared the bare bones with him, but she knew he would never understand the chaos, the lack of control, the insecurity.

How could he? He'd grown up in a palace, the pampered heir to a fortune, and he was part of a large and close family.

Correction: they were close to *him*. To her they were polite, but clearly baffled as to why someone like Ralph had chosen someone like her.

Her stomach churned.

And, judging by his behaviour, Ralph was starting to agree with them.

'Are you ready?'

She turned at his voice. Ralph was looking down at her steadily, the corners of his eyes creasing, and she felt suddenly as if the crowds had parted again and it was just the two of them, standing outside in the mid-morning sunlight.

As usual, he looked ridiculously handsome. Like every other man there he was wearing a suit—hand-made, dark, Italian design, of course—but Ralph looked nothing like any of them.

For starters—perhaps thanks to his mother's genes—he was taller. His hair was lighter too, and of course he had those incredible golden eyes.

And yet it was more than just his physical appearance that set him apart.

Around him everyone was talking expansively, hands moving, gesticulating, heads tipping back to roar with laughter, but Ralph was quiet and calm: the eye of the storm.

He had been her one place of safety—only that wasn't what she needed to be thinking right now.

'It's time to go,' he said softly.

'Yes, of course.' She nodded, then felt a rush of panic bubble up inside her as he held out his hand. But this wasn't the time or place to be proving a point and, ignoring the pulse of heat that jumped from his skin to hers as their fingers entwined, she joined the guests walking into the church.

The service followed its usual pattern, and then the priest smiled at Lucia and Luca and it was time for the christening.

Taking a breath, Juliet walked towards the font.

Although she knew it was a simple ceremony, she was slightly worried about saying her lines, but everything went perfectly. Raffaelle was utterly angelic, gazing solemnly at the priest and not even crying when the water was poured over his head.

It was beautiful, she thought, tears pricking her eyes.

And then suddenly it was over, and they were back in the midday sunshine, and everyone was smiling and clapping.

'Thank you.' Lucia was hugging her. 'Both of you.' She hugged Ralph. 'He's such a lucky boy, having two such wonderful godparents.'

Juliet smiled. 'It's an honour to be asked.'

'And you're coming in the car with us,' Lucia said firmly. 'I love my family, but after two solid days of living with my mother, my sisters and...' leaning forward, she lowered her voice, '...my *mother-in-law*, I just need a few minutes to recover.'

Tucking her arm through her friend's, Juliet laughed.

The christening reception was being held at the Casa Gregorio Hotel, twenty minutes outside of Verona. Although the word 'hotel' didn't really capture the magic of the Gregorio, Juliet thought as she slid into the cool, air-conditioned interior of the limousine.

Set in idyllic countryside, the exclusive, exquisitely renovated monastery offered a tranquil retreat from the bustle of city life, and these days the legendary kitchen garden was being put to mouth-wateringly good use by two Michelin-starred chef, Dario Bargione.

'Just sit back and enjoy the party,' she advised her friend. 'Everything is under control. You don't need to do a thing.'

Eyes suddenly bright, Lucia reached over and squeezed her hand. 'I know, and we're so grateful to you and Ralph for making this reception possible. It was so generous of you both.'

'It was our pleasure.'

Juliet felt Ralph's words skimming across her skin. You could hear it in his voice, she thought. Hundreds of years of Castellucci patronage.

How had she ever thought they would work?

Paying for Raffaelle's christening party was no big deal to him, whereas she felt uncomfortable when strangers thanked her at fundraisers and charity balls.

But then, when it came to money, the Castelluccis were in a league all their own. And, thanks to his talent for unearthing tiny start-ups that turned into commercial behemoths, Ralph had personally redefined the concept of wealth.

As well as the *palazzo* in Verona, he owned a villa in the French Riviera and penthouses in Rome, New York and London. For him money was almost irrelevant. Put simply, there was nothing he couldn't buy.

Except her.

'No, we mean it, *amico*. We can't thank you enough.' For once Luca's face was serious.

Juliet opened her mouth, but before she could speak Ralph said, 'But you have. You chose us to be godparents to Raffaelle. You're trusting us to help raise your beautiful son.' He paused. 'Aside from love, there's no gift more precious than trust. Don't you agree, *mia moglie*?'

Her heart thumped against her ribs as his eyes locked with hers. She knew he wasn't talking about Lucia and Luca.

He was talking about her.

More specifically, he was talking about her refusal to trust him, to take his word over the evidence of her eyes.

Her breath caught in her throat. *Trust.* It was such a small word and yet it encompassed so much. Confidence. Security. Hope. *And betrayal.*

Ignoring the misery filling her chest, she held his gaze.

'Ralph's right. Trust is the most precious gift.' She forced a smile onto her face. 'So thank you, both, for trusting us.'

* * *

Snatching a glass of prosecco from a passing waiter, Ralph stared across the heads of the other guests, his eyes seeking out his wife like a wolf tracking a deer.

His gaze narrowed as he caught a flash of dark red. *There she was.*

His stomach tightened.

All through the ceremony she had avoided his gaze, focusing instead on the priest and then on Raffaelle. But as she'd made her vows her eyes had met his, and suddenly he had been fighting the temptation to reach out and touch her—to press his lips against hers.

Gritting his teeth, he stared across the terrace to where his wife was talking to Luca's mother. It was a cute dress—pleated, one-shouldered, with a flippy little skirt. From a distance the print looked floral, but it was actually tiny cherries.

And then there were her shoes...

Shiny patent red heels, the colour of the Marostica cherries that grew on the hillsides in the town down the road in Vicenza.

For a moment he let his gaze drop, and felt his body hardening exponentially as his eyes drifted slowly down the length of her legs, then back up, drawn to the hollow at the back of her neck that was just visible beneath her smooth chignon.

Even now it caught him off balance. Not her looks—in his world beauty was the norm, although with that hair and face, *those legs,* it was hard not to feel as though the floor was unsteady beneath his feet—what had got under his skin that first day they'd met in Rome, and what still blew his mind even now, was how she drank in life, lived so completely in the moment.

A pulse of heat beat across his skin. Even when she was soaking wet, with her head stuck in a storm drain.

And look at her now.

Glancing across the terrace, he watched as she leaned forward to choose a canapé. He had seen her look at beautiful jewellery with the same attention and excitement. It was a quality he'd never encountered in anyone but Giulietta. The unique ability to free herself from time and place and other pressures to edit her emotions, her actions, her thoughts.

In contrast, he was both burdened with the past and preoccupied with the future. He had grown up in a world where nothing had been what it seemed. There had been mirrors that were doors, and windows that were walls, and the people had been the same.

Giulietta was different. Transparent. He had *known* her—

His mouth twisted. Except clearly he hadn't.

He watched as she caught Lucia's arm, gestured. Even at a distance it was clear that she was offering to take the baby, and his heart thumped as Raffaelle took the decision into his own hands by lunging towards his wife.

Watching her tuck the baby against her body, he felt his anger and frustration rise up inside him like mercury in a heatwave.

How could she have lied to him about wanting a baby? And why had she deceived him?

The same questions had been burning inside his head for weeks now, and he still had no answers.

Soon, he promised himself. Just a couple more hours. But first...

His shoulders tensed.

His wife was walking away from Lucia back towards the hotel.

Without so much as a beat of hesitation he began moving smoothly after her, tracking her progress through the guests mingling in the sunshine.

'Signor Castellucci?'

Ralph swore silently as Giorgio, the hotel manager, popped up beside him, smiling nervously.

'I hope you're enjoying the celebrations, *signor*. I just wanted to check that everything is to your satisfaction.'

Ralph nodded. 'It is. Thank you.' Despite his irritation, his voice was even, his smile polite.

'No, thank *you*, Signor Castellucci, for choosing Casa Gregorio for this most special of celebrations.'

Still smiling, Ralph darted his eyes over Giorgio's shoulder. If this carried on they would still be standing there thanking one another at Raffaelle's eighteenth birthday party.

'I look forward to returning very soon. Now, if you'll excuse me, I need to speak to my wife,' he said firmly.

'Ah, yes, Signora Castellucci has taken the baby to have a nap. As you requested, we have reserved a suite for that exact purpose.'

The suite was on the first floor, away from the noise of the party. He didn't need the room number. The two dark-suited bodyguards on either side of the door told him that was where he would find his wife.

He nodded to them briefly and opened the door.

After the heat of the terrace, it was blissfully cool. But it wasn't the drop in temperature that made him stop mid-step—it was the sound of his wife's voice.

She was singing softly, some kind of lullaby, and the sound was so intimate, so tender, that he felt as if he was intruding.

For a moment he almost retreated, but the softness in her voice pulled his legs forward with magnetic force.

The room was decorated in a style that might be described as 'minimalist luxe': clean lines, a neutral colour palette, and artisan furnishings with impressive ethical credentials.

A simple iron bed with a canopy of ethereal white muslin dominated the room. Through a doorway, he could see the cot that had been set up for Raffaelle.

But the baby was not in the cot.

Giulietta was holding him.

He stared at his wife in silence. Her face was soft with love and she was gazing down, entirely absorbed. Holding his breath, he stood transfixed, fury and confusion merging with desire in a maelstrom of emotion.

He was sure that he'd made no sound, and yet something made her turn towards him—and as she did so her face didn't so much change as turn to stone.

The creamy skin of her bare shoulder tugged at his gaze like a headstrong horse, and the rise of her small, rounded breasts transformed her from tender to sexy.

'What do you want?' she said hoarsely.

Behind her, a light breeze riffled the muslin, giving him a glimpse of a crisply folded sheet, and he felt his body harden with an almost unbearable hunger.

I want to take you bending over that bed, and then against the wall, and then again on that desk, didn't seem like a reply he could make.

'Luca said I need to start pulling my weight.' It wasn't quite a lie. Luca had teased him about never having changed a nappy. 'So I thought I'd see if you needed any help.' He glanced over at the sleeping baby. 'I also thought this might be an opportunity to hold him without it turning into a circus, but I can see he's settled.'

There was a moment's silence. Then, 'You can put him down if you want.'

'I'd like that,' he said quietly.

She didn't meet his eye as she handed the sleeping baby over to him, but he could feel the tension in her body as he briefly brushed against her.

Despite what Lucia had said about his size, Raffaelle seemed incredibly small and light to him. He felt his heart contract as he looked down into the baby's peach-soft untroubled face, and a primitive, unbidden instinct to protect surging through his veins.

Leaning over the cot, he gently laid the baby on his side. 'He's so perfect,' he murmured, gently touching one of the tiny thumbs.

Giulietta had followed him into the room.

'He is, isn't he?' Her eyes found his.

He smiled. 'It's hard to believe he's going to be like Luca one day.'

Personally, he thought Raffaelle looked more like

Lucia. But it was the first time she had willingly agreed with him about anything since returning to Italy, and he didn't want to lose this fragile connection between them.

'Perhaps he won't be.' She gave him a small, stiff smile. 'Not everyone grows up to be like their parents.'

She turned and walked out of the room and he stared after her, his spine tensing, picturing the handsome, patrician face of his father, Carlo Castellucci, and his mother, Francesca.

Guilt rose up inside him—guilt and shame and an anger that he couldn't seem to shift.

No, not everyone did grow up like their parents.

Blocking his mind against where that thought would lead, he followed her out of the room, leaving the door slightly ajar.

Someone had loosened the thick linen curtains, so the room was half in shade, and Giulietta had chosen to stand in the darkened half.

His chest tightened. Was that why she wanted a divorce? Did she think she could hide from him? From the truth?

'Well, in Raffaelle's case it wouldn't be a bad thing, would it?' he said.

She didn't answer, and he felt a rush of irritation.

'Is that it? You're done with the small talk?' He shook his head. 'And I thought one of your jobs as godparent was to lead by example. It's not a promising start, is it?'

Her eyes narrowed. 'It's not just small talk, Ralph. I'm done with talking to you, full-stop. And as for setting an example—I'm not sure cheating on your wife is the kind of life lesson Lucia and Luca are hoping you'll share with Raffaelle.'

Swearing softly, he crossed the room in two strides, so fast that she took a clumsy step backwards. 'For the last time, I did not cheat on you.'

'I know.'

He stared at her in confusion. 'I don't understand—'

Her eyes were fixed on his face. 'I didn't understand either at first. I thought you were lying to me. But you weren't. You're not even lying to yourself.'

She lifted her chin, and now he could see that her eyes were dark and clear with hurt and anger and determination.

'You actually believe that adultery is a part of marriage. That having a mistress doesn't cross any boundaries. But I don't think like that and I can't live like that. So can we just agree to end it here—now?'

Slowly he shook his head. 'No. Not here. Not now. Not this side of eternity, *bella.*'

Her hands curled into fists. 'But I don't want to be your wife any more.'

'*Too bad.* You see, I'm not the only one who made promises. And I'm not talking about *till death us do part.*'

He took a step closer. '*"Indivisa, etiam in morte."* The Castellucci family motto. It means "Undivided, even in death".'

Holding his breath, he pushed back the memory of his father weeping at his mother's grave.

'And that's why you want to stay married?' Giulietta asked. 'Because of some stupid medieval family motto?'

Her voice was shaking, and he could see the pulse at the base of her neck hammering against the flawless, pale skin.

'It's one of the reasons, yes.'

She was staring at him incredulously. 'Well, it's not enough. It doesn't count—it's not a real reason.'

'And that's what you want, is it?' Goaded, he closed the gap between them. 'You want something real? I'll give you real.'

And, lowering his mouth to hers, he kissed her.

He felt her body tense, her hands press against his chest, her lips part in protest—but then, even as he moved to break the kiss, her fingers were curling into his shirt and she was pulling him closer.

His hand wrapped around her waist and for a few half-seconds he was conscious of nothing but the hammering of his heart and how soft her lips were. And then he was closing the gap between them, his hand anchoring her tightly against his torso.

Oh, but she tasted so good. Soft and sweet, like *dulce de leche*. And her body was soft too…soft and pliant… so that it felt as if she was melting into him.

And where she was soft, he was hard.

Harder than he'd ever been in his life.

He groaned, sliding his fingers through her hair, his hands at her waist, pushing her up against the wall. He felt her fingers tighten in his shirt, her nails catching on the fabric as she pulled it free of his waistband, and he breathed in sharply as her hands splayed against his bare skin—

There was a sharp knock on the door.

Beneath his hands, he felt Giulietta tense.

'Excuse me, *signor*, but the nanny is here.'

He closed his eyes, wishing he could block out the bodyguard's voice as effortlessly. *Not now.*

But it was too late. His wife was pushing away from him, smoothing her hair back from her face in a gesture that was an unmistakable shorthand for *We're done here.*

'Giulietta—'

He reached for her, but she sidestepped him with such speed and agility that he was still tucking in his shirt when he heard the door open and her voice telling the nanny to 'go on in'.

Breathing shakily, Juliet pulled out her phone and checked the time. The taxi firm had said twenty past and it was a quarter past now.

Her heart felt as though it was going to burst through her ribcage.

What had she said to Ralph? *'Not everyone grows up to be like their parents.'*

Obviously *she* had.

She moaned softly. Wasn't it bad enough that she had let Ralph kiss her? Had she had to kiss him back?

Remembering how she had pulled at his shirt, how her hands had pressed against his skin, she felt her face grow hot.

And not just kiss him...

Quelling a bout of panic, she checked her phone again. Just one minute to go. And then this would all be over.

Her flight wasn't for another three hours, but once she was at the airport she could check in and then— She felt her pulse accelerate.

Oh, thank goodness. It was here. The taxi was here.

Holding up her hand in greeting, she watched, relief flooding through her, as the car came to a halt.

'*Ciao.* The airport, please.'

She opened the door—but as she leaned into the taxi a hand closed over her wrist.

'Not so fast.'

In one smooth movement Ralph had slammed the door and pulled her away from the car.

The next moment one of the bodyguards stepped forward, bending down to the driver's window. Before she'd even had a chance to open her mouth in protest the taxi had sped off.

She shook herself free. 'What do you think you're playing at?'

His face was impassive, but there was a dangerous glitter in his eyes. 'I could ask you the same question. Only there's no need. You're making quite a habit of this, *bella.* Sneaking off without saying goodbye.'

He was right. She was sneaking off. But how could she have stayed after what had just happened? After what she'd let happen?

'It's got nothing to do with you.'

'Wrong. You're my wife. I think you sneaking away from a christening party for *our* godson has got every-thing to do with me.' He shook his head in mute frus-tration. 'How do you think Lucia and Luca would feel when they realised?'

Her stomach twisted with guilt. She couldn't meet his eye. Of course she had wanted to say goodbye—but then she would have had to tell them that she was leaving Italy for good.

'They'd understand,' she said, cringing inside at how callous she sounded.

He clearly thought so too; the contempt on his face made hot tears burn the back of her eyes.

She took a step backwards. But how dare he try to shame her? 'You know what, Ralph? You're so keen to keep reminding me that I'm your wife, but maybe if you hadn't forgotten that you're my husband this wouldn't be happening.'

His face hardened. 'Really? You want to do this now? Here?'

'I don't want to do it anywhere,' she snapped. 'I want to go the airport.'

He was staring at her as if she had said she wanted to go to the outer ring of Saturn.

'You want to leave? You want to go back to England? After what just happened?'

Her pulse accelerated. 'Why wouldn't I? What happened didn't change anything.'

He swore softly. 'I kissed you. And you kissed me back. You wanted a reason to stay and I gave you one.'

She felt pinpricks of heat sweep over her body. 'Well, you probably confused me with someone else. Like your mistress. I certainly confused you with someone else. Someone with scruples. Someone who wasn't going to lie to my face.'

'I'm not lying,' he said quietly.

She watched, frozen with misery, as he lifted his hand and, seemingly out of nowhere, a familiar sleek dark limousine drew up beside them. A second car followed a beat behind.

'Please get in the car, Giulietta.'

Planting her feet firmly on the Tarmac, she lifted her chin. 'I told you—I'm going to the airport.'

A muscle flickered along his jawline. 'Fine. My car is here, ready and waiting.'

She straightened her back. 'And it'll carry on waiting unless you tell me who she is.'

'I've told you she's no threat.' His voice was expressionless.

'Just tell me. Do you love her?'

His silence wrapped around her throat, choking her. She couldn't breathe. The ache in her chest was swallowing her whole. No pain had ever felt like it.

Suddenly she felt exhausted. It was over. All this was just her fighting the inevitable. Fighting the knowledge that she was the problem. She had failed as a daughter, and now she had failed as a wife.

But she couldn't fight any more. She was done.

'Goodbye, then, Ralph.'

She spun on her heel, but as she started to walk away he blocked her path.

'She's not a threat,' he said again. And then he closed his eyes, as if he too had stopped fighting.

Suddenly she didn't want to hear the truth. She didn't want to hear about this woman who had captured his heart and broken hers.

'Don't, Ralph, please...' she whispered, turning away.

Swearing softly, he spun her round, his hand tipping up her chin. 'She's not my mistress. She's my sister.'

She looked at him for one long, excruciating moment and then she pushed his hand away. 'You don't have a sister.' She shook her head, rage mingling with misery. 'You don't have any siblings.'

His skin was stretched taut over his cheekbones, like a canvas on a frame. 'She's my half-sister.'

Half-sister.

She stared at him mutely. That couldn't be true—but why lie?

'What's her name?'

He hesitated, then sighed. 'Vittoria. Her name's Vittoria Farnese.'

She felt a rush of confusion, almost like vertigo. The name sounded familiar.

'So why hasn't anyone mentioned her?' Her tone was accusatory. 'Or am I supposed to believe your entire family is suffering from some kind of collective amnesia?'

'They don't know about her.'

There was tension in his frame now, as though speaking each sentence required an effort of will.

She looked at his face, trying to fill in the gaps, to make sense out of what made no sense at all, unless… 'Are you saying—do you mean Carlo had an affair?'

He shook his head. 'It was my mother. She had the affair.'

Her heart hammered against her ribs. 'So Vittoria is her daughter?'

There was a stretch of silence and then he shook

his head again. 'No, Vittoria is my half-sister on my father's side.'

He stared past her, letting his words sink in.

'But you said your father didn't have an affair...' she said slowly.

'He didn't.'

And now she could hear the pain in his voice.

'But Carlo Castellucci is not my biological father.'

CHAPTER FOUR

FOR THE SECOND time in less than twenty-four hours Juliet found herself climbing into the limousine on automatic pilot. But this time it was not so much habit that propelled her as shock.

She watched numbly as Ralph leaned into the driver's side window to talk to Marco. Her head was spinning. Questions were bubbling inside her so fast and so violently that she felt as though a dam had burst and she was being carried along in the surging water.

Breathing out shakily, she tried to put her thoughts in some kind of order—but it was hard to do that when she felt as though she'd been kicked in the stomach.

Her fingers tightened around the smooth leather armrest as Ralph sat down beside her. She was stunned… confounded by what Ralph had told her. But most of all she felt swamped with guilt for not having been there for him.

For weeks now, she had been so sure that he was having an affair. And, given that she'd spent most of her married life waiting for their relationship to fall apart, it had been easy to stay sure even when he'd denied her accusations repeatedly.

Her pulse shivered.

Easy to convince herself that his denial was simply the reflex of a wealthy man not used to having to justify his actions. After all, the Castellucci male's right to variety in his marriage was not just hearsay. It was well-documented in art and history.

But if what he said was true then she was wrong.

Her husband hadn't been unfaithful.

She breathed in against a sharp rush of adrenaline.

And, perhaps more shockingly, Carlo was not his father.

Glancing at Ralph's set face, she felt her heart begin hammering inside her chest.

And as the silence stretched out in the air-conditioned chill of the limo she knew there were no 'ifs' or 'buts' about it.

It was true.

She could see it in the tension around his jawline and the rigidity in his shoulders.

And in that moment her own anger and hurt were instantly superseded by the emotions she knew her husband must be feeling.

How had he discovered the truth?

And who was his real father?

Gritting her teeth against the weight of questions forming in her throat, she said quietly, 'When did you find out?'

His hesitation was so brief she might not have registered it had it not been for the slight tensing around his eyes. Then he turned to face her.

'My mother told me. Not long before she died.' His eyes locked with hers. 'She'd wanted to tell me sooner, only she never found the right time.' Pain, mostly masked, shimmered for a moment. 'I think she realised she'd run out of time.'

Juliet stared at him mutely, the strain in his voice pinching her heart. She'd had difficult conversations with her own mother—the last one in particular had been in a class of its own. The only positive was that she had initiated it, so that the time and place had been of her choosing.

Pushing aside the memory of that appalling day, she said hesitantly, 'Does anyone else know? Does your father—?' She stumbled over the word. 'Sorry. I mean, does Carlo know?'

Carlo Castellucci.

She could still remember the first time she had met her father-in-law. Her stomach lurched at the memory. Would it have been any less intimidating if she'd known then what she knew now?

Probably not, she concluded. At the time she'd been dazed—dazzled, really—by the glamour of the Castelluccis and the lives they led. And as the resident patriarch of the family, Carlo's unlined face and languid, cocktail party smile had perfectly embodied that glamour.

He had kissed her on both cheeks, welcomed her to the family, but despite his words she had sensed his well-bred disbelief.

Her hands curled in her lap, her fingers grazing the huge yellow diamond that Ralph had given her to make up for the lack of an engagement ring.

Part of her hadn't blamed Carlo. After all, Ralph was his adored son. Only now it appeared that he wasn't.

She felt again that same shock of something fundamental being turned on its head, like a storm of hailstones beating down on a sunny beach in July.

Her heartbeat stuttered as Ralph shook his head.

'No one knows except me and Vittoria. And now you. My mother didn't—' his jaw tightened '—couldn't tell my father.' His voice sounded as if it was scraping over gravel. 'She knew how much it would hurt him. '

'And she didn't think it would hurt you?'

The words were out of her mouth before she could stop them, propelled by a spasm of anger that had nothing to do with Francesca Castellucci's infidelity. It was an anger that came from having had to deal with adult truths at an age when she had been ill-equipped to deal with them.

Chest tightening, she smoothed a crease from the skirt of her dress. But when would any child be ready for something like this? It was the most basic, essential truth—one you unthinkingly took for granted. Your mother and father were your parents. To learn that was a lie…

His expression didn't change, but something flickered in his eyes. 'She thought it was important that I knew the truth.'

Now Juliet felt a sharp pang of empathy for Francesca. Telling the truth sounded so easy. All you had to do was say what was in your head or your heart. But countless family therapy sessions had taught her that it was a whole lot more complicated than just opening your mouth and talking.

In practice, it was more like balancing an equation—facts had to be weighed up against the feelings they inspired, and often the process had to be done in the blink of an eye.

She watched as Ralph glanced away to where the sun was starting to dip down into the hills. His head didn't move. 'She wanted to give me the chance to get to know my biological father, Niccolò Farnese. If that was what I wanted.'

And was it?

A sudden silence filled the space between them. Inside her head, her heartbeat was deafeningly loud as a mix of panic and misery mingled uneasily in her stomach.

Once she'd thought she knew instinctively what Ralph wanted, but for months now she'd had no idea what he was thinking, and she didn't understand what mattered to him or why. It was as if there was some invisible barrier between them, blocking that immutable private bond they had once shared.

Correction: that she'd *thought* they had once shared.

She took a breath, needing to process her thoughts, his words.

Niccolò Farnese. That name was definitely familiar, and now she was putting a face to the name...the face of a handsome, smiling man, waving to the crowds...

She stared at Ralph, the image frozen in her head.

'Are we talking about Niccolò Farnese the politician?' Politician, philanthropist and media tycoon.

He nodded. 'We are.'

His slightly accented voice was quiet, but firm. He had a beautiful voice...

Glancing at his profile, she felt her breath tangle in her throat. Before bumping into Ralph in Rome, she'd spent a few days on her own, exploring the city. Rome was bursting with things to see and do, and she had devoured all the sights as greedily as she had the *supplì*—the deep-fried rice croquettes sold in pizzerias across the capital.

It was truly the eternal city. Everywhere she'd looked she had seen ancient ruins rubbing up against modern concrete curves. She had been smitten...speechless. But it had been the ceiling of the Sistine Chapel that had left her reeling. It was mesmerisingly beautiful. Each time she'd looked up, something else had held her captive.

Her eyes fluttered across the car. Only in comparison to Ralph even the artistic power and brilliance of Michelangelo felt muted. He was so close, so solid beside her...

She breathed in and felt her stomach muscles tighten, responding to the pull of his beauty and the hint of leashed power. Her body was remembering the feel of his mouth on hers, the way he kissed, touched, caressed—

Her heart began beating unsteadily.

And he hadn't been unfaithful.

She reached across the seat and took his hand, felt a

pulse of hope ticking over her skin as his fingers tightened on hers.

Maybe she'd had to push him, kicking and screaming, into doing so, but he was talking to her now—talking in a way that he had never done before.

Her pulse dipped. Her marriage wasn't over. They could work this out.

She squeezed his hand. 'And is it what you want? To get to know him? Niccolò?'

He made an impatient sound. 'You don't need to worry about that.'

'But what if I did?'

His features tightened. 'I wouldn't tell you. This is my problem and I will find a solution.'

He looked across the car but his expression was distant—as if he wasn't really seeing her. Watching him lean back in his seat, she felt her a trickle of ice run down her spine. He might not be Carlo Castellucci's biological son, she thought dully, but the casual dismissal in his voice was a pitch-perfect match of the man who had raised him.

Replaying his words in her head, she felt her mouth tighten. Surely he wasn't being serious? They needed to talk about this. Didn't he want to talk to her about this? She was his wife…

For a few half-seconds she thought back to their wedding ceremony and how his eyes had meshed with hers as he slid the single gold band onto her finger.

Her throat tightened and she thought of the blind, limitless happiness of their wedding day bleaching out to nothing.

She might be his wife, but he couldn't make his message any clearer short of parading in front of her with a placard.

As far as he was concerned, she knew *enough*. Everything else was beyond her pay grade.

He'd given her the basic facts, just as he might to a child. But she wasn't a child. She was an idiot.

A chill was creeping over her skin, and with it the unwelcome but inescapable awareness that, far from being a turning point in their relationship, this was simply another example of how far apart they were.

His confession had never been about confiding in her. It had been an exercise in damage limitation.

Glancing helplessly down at her hands, she took a deep breath, hating him, and hating herself for being so naive as to think that he could change…that he even *wanted* to change.

'You're right,' she said. Smiling thinly, she slipped her hand free of his. 'It's none of my business.'

She stared down at her dress, remembering how she had smoothed out the pretty cherry-printed fabric just before the sky fell in. Just before it had become clear that he was willing to commit them both to this marriage for no better reason than—what? Pride? The need to maintain a public façade?

She was done with this. With him. There were no more questions she needed or wanted to have answered. Not any more. And not because she didn't care, but because she did. And it was too dangerous to let herself keep caring about this beautiful, baffling man.

Caring was a hoax. Her parents had taught her that.

It was a game played by the heart to distract the head from looking too closely at the facts. Or, in this case, one diamond-hard fact that she had chosen to ignore.

Her fears about Ralph's infidelity had simply been a distraction from the bigger picture. From their fundamentally different beliefs about what made a happy, healthy marriage.

She felt the car slow.

Outside, the sounds of the real world bumped against the solid body of the car. Men shouting…some kind of machinery humming…

As she looked up, her eyes clashed with his.

He raised an eyebrow. 'None of your business, *bella*? How so? You're my wife.'

So now she was his wife?

She could feel anger rising in waves inside her. Marriage was supposed to be a partnership of equals. But with Ralph everything had to be played out on his terms. He got to make the rules and change them as and when it suited him to do so.

Catching sight of her wedding band, she felt her heart being squeezed as though by a fist. She'd kept it on, telling herself that she had to for appearances' sake. But the truth was that, despite telling him she wanted a divorce, a part of her had still been hoping that she could make her marriage work.

Now, though, she knew nothing she did or said could make that happen.

She forced herself to speak past the frustration twisting in her throat. 'Fat lot of difference that makes.'

His golden gaze bored into her. 'Meaning?'

'Meaning that wives are not just for sex and providing heirs. Not this wife, anyway. So when I get back to England I will be filing for divorce.'

She reached for her wedding ring, struggling to loosen it from her finger.

His hand covered hers. 'Leave it on.

Pulling her hand free, she glared at him. 'Why? I'm not staying married to you, Ralph.'

Tilting his head back, he stared at her in silence. The silence stretched and stretched, and when finally he spoke she could hear a note of exasperation in his voice.

'Enough of this, Giulietta.' His voice rose. *'Enough.'*

He made a gesture that was familiar to her. It was the same gesture he made in a restaurant, when he dismissed a waiter. Like waving away a particularly persistent fly.

'There will be no divorce—as you very well know. You made accusations and you were wrong. But fortunately for you I'm willing to forget your behaviour.'

She gaped at him mutely, a ripple of anger, smooth and hot like lava, snaking sideways across her skin. 'Well, I'm not willing to forget yours,' she said slowly.

His gaze was direct and unwavering. 'Did you not understand anything of what I just told you? I haven't been having an affair—'

'I know.' She cut him off. 'And I'm sorry that I thought you were. But it doesn't make any difference—'

Now he cut her off. 'You're kidding me?' His mouth curved upwards at the corners, but there was nothing humorous about his smile.

As she started to shake her head he pressed his hand

against his eyes, as if doing so might change what he was seeing.

'Let me get this right. You spend days accusing me of being unfaithful with another woman. Not only that, you storm off to England for *five weeks* because you need "space".'

His voice was quiet—soft, even—but it crackled with an authority that made it impossible for her to look away.

'According to you, nothing I say or do matters except the truth. So I tell you the truth. Only now you're saying it makes no difference.'

He practically chewed the words and spat them out at her.

'It doesn't…'

Her heart was racing with panic and pain. He was right. When she'd gone to London she'd thought all she cared about was finding out for certain if he was having an affair. Threatening to divorce him had been the only thing she could think of that would push him into telling the truth.

But in these last few minutes she'd finally accepted that what they'd shared had never been strong enough to survive outside of that small hotel room in Rome.

Marriages needed solid foundations.

They needed transparency and trust.

Ralph didn't trust her, and she sure as hell didn't trust him.

Not with her heart or her future.

Nor could she risk giving him a second chance—not when she knew first-hand how easy it was for that second chance to slip into a third, and then another and another.

But one look at his face told her that trying to explain that to this man would be a fruitless exercise.

'There's no point in trying to do this here...now. Let's leave it to the lawyers.'

Ralph would have access to some of the finest legal brains in the world, but she had everything she needed with her. Her passport was in her handbag. She wanted nothing from the house. Her broken heart was all the reminder she needed of her failed marriage.

As she opened the car door she heard him call her name, sensed him reaching out for her.

But it was too late.

It had always been too late.

Stepping out onto the kerb, she froze, her mouth hanging open. She had been so preoccupied by their conversation that she had barely glanced out of the window during the journey, but naturally she'd assumed they were heading to the airport.

But they were not at the airport.

Nor were they in Verona.

They were at the marina in Venice.

She gazed up at the huge, gleaming white yacht, her skin prickling with shock and disbelief.

Not just any yacht.

Ralph's yacht. The *Alighieri*.

Ralph had got out of the car.

She spun round to face him, a wave of fury cascading through her body. 'You said you were taking me to the airport.'

He shook his head. 'I think you'll find that I didn't. Besides, why would you want to leave now? We're in the middle of a conversation.'

'We are not in the middle of anything. We are at the end,' she snapped.

Her voice was rising, and on the other side of the road a couple of men loading equipment onto another boat turned towards her, their eyes sharp with curiosity.

'So, unless you want me to cause a truly memorable scene that will make your illustrious ancestors roll over in their graves, I suggest you take me back to Verona right now.'

Although she knew there was every chance she would miss her flight...

'That's not going to happen.'

His face was impassive, and his cool, untroubled expression made her want to scream.

Stomach curling with apprehension, she glared at him. 'I'm warning you, Ralph. I won't hold back.'

He stared at her for a long moment, his golden eyes locking with hers. 'Oh, I know, *bella*,' he said softly. 'You're always very vocal...'

She felt her breath catch, her pulse fluttering. Ralph knew exactly how to make her lose control.

Only she didn't need reminding of that now.

'We're not doing this, Ralph,' she said stiffly.

'Really?' He raised one smooth dark eyebrow. 'I thought you weren't going to hold back?'

His eyes gleamed with the satisfaction of having proved a point, and suddenly she hated him more than she had ever hated anyone.

How did he always manage to make it so that she ended up on the wrong foot? If only for once she could get under his skin, make him see red, lose his head, lose control…

But she didn't have to stand here and wait for him to stop playing his silly games. She was perfectly capable of getting herself back to Verona. Alone.

She spun round, but as she started to walk away, he blocked her path.

'We need to talk,' he said softly.

He sounded calm, but there was something flickering in the dark gold gaze. Like a warning beam from a lighthouse. *Danger. Rocks ahead.*

But she was too awash with misery and humiliation to care. 'I gave you a chance to talk and you threw it in my face.' Her eyes narrowed, her body vibrating from the close proximity to his. 'And, frankly, I don't have anything left to say to you,' she hissed.

'That suits me fine.' His voice was infuriatingly calm. 'It means I can talk without interruption.'

And, without missing a beat, he plucked her handbag from her fingers, tossed it to his bodyguard and scooped her up into his arms.

Gritting his teeth, Ralph ignored his wife's flailing fists and, shifting her body, tipped her over his shoulder.

'Put me down!'

'Oh, I will—just as soon as you're safely on deck.'

She had threatened to make a scene. If that was what she wanted, then that was what she was going to get, he thought savagely, tightening his grip.

'Let me go! You can't do this!'

'Apparently I can,' he said softly.

After he'd stepped on deck he moved swiftly through the boat, nodding briskly at Franco, the skipper, and the crew members.

They reached the master cabin and he walked across the room and dropped her onto the bed.

She swore graphically.

He frowned. 'I'm not sure if that's anatomically possible.'

From somewhere down below a low hum rose up through the boat as the engines started.

Her eyes narrowed as she looked past his shoulder at the open door.

'Don't!' he said warningly.

'Or what?' she raged. 'You're already kidnapping me.'

He shrugged. 'I'm not asking for a ransom, so technically it's more of an abduction—'

As she swore again, he watched her, like a cat with a mouse.

Actually, he thought, this was retribution. It was payback for the hypocrisy of her behaviour. She had no idea what she had put him through these last few weeks, but she was going to find out now.

Her chin lifted pugnaciously, and despite his own simmering anger he couldn't but admire her defiance. And the indignant swell of her high-riding breasts...

'You had this coming, *bella*.'

'Why? For having the temerity to want more than you're offering?'

Fighting an urge to pick her up again and toss her overboard, he narrowed his eyes. Was she serious? Was that what this was about?

'You live in a palace,' he said coolly. 'You have access to a private jet, this yacht, a limousine. You have an unlimited expense account. Do you know what most women would give to have your life?'

'Well, they can have it—and you.' She glared up at him. 'There's more to life and marriage than palaces and private jets, Ralph.'

Yes, there was. A whole lot more.

Her soft brown eyes were muddied with anger and resentment, and the set of her jaw held more or less the same message as her eyes. But, glancing down at her, he felt his heartbeat quicken and his groin tighten.

Probably it was her hair, he thought distractedly. Gone was the smooth chignon. Now her long tawny hair fell about her shoulders in disarray. Like it did in bed. When she rode him. Head thrown back, small upturned breasts bared to his gaze, face taut with the fierce, animal passion that would melt away into surrender at the moment of climax.

He felt his breath catch.

In the time it had taken for his brain to conjure up that picture, his body had hardened as if in a forge, and the speed at which his anger had turned to hunger did little to improve his temper.

Ignoring the ache in his groin, he stared at her steadily. 'Like what?'

She scrambled to her feet, her glossy hair fanning out behind her. 'Like honesty.'

Honesty?

The word vibrated in his head.

Ma che cazzo!

His fingers twitched. He wanted to shake her. Or kiss her. Maybe both.

How could she look him in the eye and talk about honesty? She had been lying to him for months. Not in words, maybe. But in her actions. Pretending that they were trying for a baby when she'd known the whole time that it would never happen.

He took a step towards her. 'I have been honest with you. I have told you about Vittoria.'

And she had no understanding of how hard that had been. How impossible it had been to say the words out loud.

His family were not like other families. The Castellucci name was not just a name, it was a brand. They lived in the public eye. Every birth, marriage and death was given round-the-clock news coverage and everything in between was meticulously managed.

And this scandal would not just be about him, but his entire family.

He had kept the secret to himself to protect the people he loved most in the world and he'd been so careful.

But then Giulietta had seen him with Vittoria. And it hadn't mattered what he'd said—she wouldn't let it go.

She should have trusted him. Like he'd trusted her.

His pulse twitched and he thought about the empty blister packet in his pocket. He'd been carrying it around with him for months now—carrying around the pain and shock of her deceit, waiting to confront her as she had confronted him.

She was staring at him, her lush eyelashes flaring around her widened eyes.

'Only because I made you tell me,' she said.

Her hands were clenched—not into fists, but as if she were trying to hold on to something.

'I don't understand…' The words sounded as if they were caught in her throat. 'You're acting like there's some kind of need-to-know basis and I don't have clearance.'

The catch in her voice snagged at something in his chest. He had hurt her, and he didn't like how that made him feel. But she was wrong. He had been planning to tell her the truth.

Not at the beginning—not when they'd first met in Rome. Later, though, in those first few months of their marriage, the honeymoon period, he'd fully intended to tell her. Only each time something had happened. First Carlo had been rushed to hospital with a kidney infection, and then Raffaelle had been born by emergency C-section.

For a split second he replayed the moment when he'd noticed the gleam of silver in the bin, remembering his confusion, and then the headrush of shock, the pain of betrayal.

Another betrayal.

And this one worse, somehow, for not being refracted through his father.

After that there had been no way he could trust her with the truth about his parentage.

His throat tightened. He still didn't understand why she'd done it. Why mislead him like that? Why let him think they were trying for a baby?

He thought back to that moment in the hotel when he had seen her holding Raffaelle. It had been like a painting brought to life, everything in the room retreating so that it was just the woman and the child illuminated in the early evening sunlight.

Her gaze had been fixed on Raffaelle's face, her eyes soft with love and longing, and in that moment he had known with absolute conviction that she wanted a baby of her own.

But that meant there was only one possible explanation for why she had been taking the contraceptive pill.

His fingers curled into fists. She didn't want a baby with *him*.

Had that been how his mother had felt about Carlo?

Having realised too late that she'd married the wrong man, had she deliberately chosen to get pregnant? To keep a piece of her lover for herself?

The thought of Giulietta having a baby with another man made him want to smash the cabin to pieces with his bare hands.

'What else is there to know?' he asked. His voice echoed harshly round the room, but anger had stifled all other emotions.

'What else?' she repeated. 'Oh, I don't know, Ralph… How about what you're thinking. What you're feeling.'

His feelings. He felt his chest tighten. *No way*.

To share how it had felt to have his whole life upended, to watch history being redacted and rewritten? His history?

Ever since that day it had felt as if he was walking through a minefield. Every step carried an unseen risk. Nothing was what it seemed. Looking at his reflection, he felt like an imposter. An actor hired to play Ralph Castellucci.

The one constant in this storm of uncertainty should have been Giulietta and the child they would make together. Her child and his. Only now, thanks to his wife, it turned out that his dreams for the future were as shifting and ephemeral as his past.

And now she wanted him to share his feelings.

His jaw tightened. Why shouldn't he let her know what it felt like to be kept in the dark? 'I don't know what benefit that would serve.'

She was staring at him, her eyes blazing.

'But that's not what marriage is about, Ralph. You can't choose which parts of yourself you get to share. We're a couple. We're supposed to share everything—especially the truth.'

'It's good advice.' His eyes locked with hers. 'What a pity you don't apply it to yourself.'

She stared at him, the pulse in her throat leaping against her skin like a startled rabbit. 'I don't know what you're talking about.'

'You don't?' He reached into his pocket. 'Then allow me to refresh your memory.'

Stalking towards her, he tossed the blister pack onto the bed.

'These were in the bin in our bathroom.'

He watched her face stiffen with shock.

'You want to talk about honesty, *bella*? Then perhaps you'd like to explain why you've been *pretending* to try for a baby for months.'

CHAPTER FIVE

JULIET STARED AT Ralph in silence.

Shock was clawing at her, swamping her. Beneath her feet she could feel the *Alighieri* moving smoothly through the lagoon. Soon it would reach the choppier waters of the Adriatic, but she was already adrift and starting to drown in a treacherous sea of her own making.

She tried to speak, but her throat was dry and choked.

Heart pummelling her ribs, she glanced down at the packet. There were empty spaces where the pills had once been and now they gazed back at her like twenty-eight accusing eyes.

In her head, she had rationalised her behaviour. She had got married in haste to a man who had turned from soul mate to stranger in front of her eyes. It had broken her heart, but she'd decided she could, and would, live with her mistake.

But, no matter how badly she'd wanted a baby, she couldn't allow herself to bring a child into the world.

How could she? When every day she had felt herself and Ralph slipping further apart from each other?

Watched the pure white brilliance of their love fading into darkness like a dying star?

Only now, faced with his real and justifiable anger, she felt her certainty fade. 'I can explain—'

'You said you wanted a baby.' His eyes narrowed and the cabin seemed to shrink in on her as he took a step closer. 'We talked about it three months ago and we decided that it was the right time. *We* decided that, Giulietta—not me. You said it was what you wanted.'

His hands—those beautiful long-fingered hands that had made pleasure pulse through her body—clenched at his sides. She swallowed past her panic, ripples of guilt spreading out over her skin like the wake from the *Alighieri*.

They had talked about having children.

She could remember the conversation almost word for word. It had been the exact opposite of the conversation they were having now. Easy, smooth-flowing, punctuated by laughter and smiles and kisses. So many kisses… Warm, sweet, soft at first, then more urgent, the heat of his lips demanding a response she had been more than happy to give, her body melting against his…

She pushed the memory away.

'I know I did. And it was what I wanted…' She faltered, her voice dropping.

It still is, she thought, an ache spreading through her chest. Holding Raffaelle at the christening party had been both a joy and an agony. But, if anything, she and Ralph were further apart now than they had ever been— like the earth from the sun at aphelion in its orbit.

He frowned down at her. 'Strange, then, that you

would carry on taking a pill whose sole purpose is to stop that happening.'

His voice was rough-sounding, but it was the serrated edge to his gaze that made her skin feel as though it was being flayed from her body.

'I'm sorry.'

She meant it. She'd hated misleading him. But her words sounded meagre and inadequate even to her. As if she was speaking by rote, not from the heart.

Ralph clearly thought so too.

He swore beneath his breath. 'For what?' he asked abruptly. He was staring at her in disbelief, his handsome face harsh in the fading light of the cabin. 'For deceiving me for months? Lying to me?'

Her heart was pounding and she could barely breathe. The diamond ring on her finger felt like a leaden band.

'I didn't lie.'

He stared at her for a long time, as if he didn't know who she was. 'Only because I didn't actually ask if you'd come off the pill,' he said slowly. 'Idiot that I am, I didn't think I needed to. I just assumed you had.' His gaze didn't waver. 'Just out of interest, would you have told me the truth if I'd asked?'

How could she explain?

How could she put into words how she had felt?

The sliding panic, the sense of losing her grip, spinning out of control, and the creeping dread of knowing that she was moments away from impact but powerless to stop it.

To have done so would have meant talking about a life she had not just abandoned, but buried. It would have meant confessing more secrets, more lies—or 'unspoken truths' as she preferred to think of them.

When could she have told him about Juliet Jones? The small, scared, brittle child who had waited in her bedroom for the shouting to stop and waited in the playground, hoping someone would remember to pick her up after school. How could she have explained about living in a house where there had always been alcohol but no food?

She shivered inside.

Talking about it would have made it feel real again, and she couldn't have coped with that. That was why she'd fled to England five weeks ago. To put as much distance as possible between herself and those feelings.

'I don't know,' she said quietly.

There was another silence, thick and heavy like the silence that preceded a storm.

He took a breath, ran a hand over his face, swallowed.

For a moment she thought he was trying to think of a suitable response, but when finally he looked at her again she knew why he'd hesitated.

He hadn't been thinking. He was just too angry to speak. Not just angry, but coldly furious and barely hiding it.

She tried again. 'I didn't mean—'

'Di che diavolo parli!'

This time he swore out loud, and the anger in his voice sliced through the panicky drumroll of her heartbeat.

'"I didn't mean to" doesn't fly in this situation. You were taking a contraceptive pill. Fifty-six pills, in fact.

That wasn't an accident or a mistake, Giulietta. It was deliberate.'

A dark flush of anger was highlighting his beautiful curving cheekbones.

'You didn't want to be pregnant.'

He shook his head.

'All these weeks you've been sitting in judgement of me, accusing me of being dishonest, when all the time you were playing me for a fool. You're such a hypocrite.'

Her breath caught in her throat. She took a step backwards, her panic giving way to anger. 'That's not fair,' she said, stung by his words, by their truth and their injustice.

His face was a hard mask. 'No, what's not fair is making me believe there was a chance you might be pregnant when you knew definitively that there couldn't be.'

She flinched inwardly. He was right, but he was ignoring his part in why she'd acted that way.

'I did want a baby when we talked about it.' Her fingers curled into her palms. 'But then everything changed. You changed.'

Even before she had seen him with Vittoria he had become different. Gone had been the man who had taken her to the Trevi Fountain to watch the sun rise over the city and then produced a breakfast picnic of *maritozzo* and *ciambella* with fresh cherries.

They hadn't been able to get enough of each other...

But then everything had begun to change. Her husband had never been at home, and when he had been they'd hardly spoken.

His eyes were dark with frustration. 'So it's my fault you lied?'

She stared at him. 'No, that's not what I'm saying. I'm trying to tell you how it was. How we ended up like this.'

Her voice was rising now, and the tension and unhappiness of the last few weeks was enveloping her. It felt as if she was playing snakes and ladders—a game she loathed. Every time they seemed to be getting somewhere she landed on a snake and went slipping back to the start.

They would never sort this out.

The only way they had ever managed to communicate successfully was physically.

But sex couldn't resolve anything but lust.

Nor would having a baby tackle the raw emotions and complex issues they'd spent months circumnavigating.

A lump formed in her throat. 'You're not the man I married, Ralph.'

The silence tautened between them. Heart pounding, she watched his shoulders tense. There was a strange light in his eyes and his breathing wasn't quite steady.

'Finally,' he said quietly, 'we have something we can agree on.'

And before she could react, much less form a sentence, he turned and strode through the door.

Walking back through the boat, Ralph thought his hammering heart was going to break through his ribcage. He had waited so long to confront Giulietta, only nothing had gone according to plan. In fact, he couldn't have handled it any worse if he'd set out to do so.

In his head he'd played out various scenarios, and in all of them he'd stayed calm, coolly presenting the facts of her betrayal like a prosecuting lawyer. But the last forty-eight hours had made staying cool an impossibility.

His shoulders tensed.

More specifically, *his wife* had made staying cool impossible on so many levels.

He wasn't sure if it was her continued insistence that they get a divorce or the fact that after five weeks of abstinence his body was in a state of almost permanent discomfort, but as he'd carried her on board all his good intentions had been swept away by a toppling wave of anger.

It had been like nothing he'd ever known—a feeling so pure and absolute it had wiped out everything: all dignity and decorum and understanding.

His chest tightened.

He'd wanted answers, not a screaming match. He'd failed on both counts.

His stomach was tight, and aching as if he was hungry, but when he walked out onto the spacious on-deck lounge area he headed to the bar.

Leaning over the marble countertop, he reached for a bottle of his favourite whisky—a thirty-year-old single malt Laphroaig.

But maybe he should eat.

He glanced at the intercom. It would be no trouble to call downstairs and get the chef to prepare him a light supper. Then again, after his performance earlier the crew were probably hiding in the lifeboats.

And he also knew the ache in his stomach had nothing to do with lack of food. It had been there since Giulietta had fled from the *palazzo*.

Pushing aside the memory of that night, he snatched up a tumbler and made his way over to one of the huge sofas. His wife might be the most infuriating woman on the planet, but he wasn't quite at the necking-it-from-the-bottle stage yet.

He unscrewed the top of the bottle, poured out two fingers of whisky and drank it in one gulp. It was a crime not to savour it, but right now he needed the hit of alcohol to dull his senses and the feeling of failure.

Then, maybe, he might be able to think about—

He frowned. What was it she had said? Oh, yes—how they had ended up like this.

Gritting his teeth, he poured another glass. This time, though, he rested it on the arm of the sofa.

Who was it who had said that people lost things that they wanted to lose? For him, meeting Giulietta in Rome had been the opposite. He had found the one woman he'd wanted to find.

Beautiful, smart, and free from the expectations of the world he lived in, she had wanted him for himself. Not for his wealth or his name or his connections. For her, he had been enough.

Or so he'd thought.

He still couldn't accept that he had got it wrong. But it wasn't just up to him.

His fingers tightened around the glass and he had to stop himself from tipping the contents down his throat.

'You're not the man I married.'

He breathed out unsteadily, her words replaying in his head. Had he changed? Yes and no.

When they'd met in Rome it had been a little over five months since his mother's deathbed confession. Six months since Vittoria had come to the house and tearfully confronted him with the letters she'd found.

His heart began beating faster. Love letters from *his* mother, Francesca, to *her* father, Niccolò. Intense, passion-filled letters that he'd struggled to read but found impossible to ignore. Particularly the one in which she begged Niccolò to meet her so that she could tell him her news.

At first his mother had refused to discuss it. It had only been in those last few days that she had finally confirmed what was hinted at in the letters.

Niccolò, not Carlo, was his father.

His mouth twisted.

And ever since then he'd been trying to decide what to do next. That was what the trip to Rome had been about. Getting some space from the family, from Verona, from the life that had been mapped out for him as heir-in-waiting to the Castellucci empire.

He'd wanted—needed—to do the right thing. The trouble was that then he hadn't been sure what that was. He still wasn't.

Saying nothing to Carlo was the simplest option— only that would mean living a lie for the rest of his life.

On the other hand, telling the truth would have devastating consequences.

The Castellucci name would be lost. Worse, the man who had raised him from birth and earned the right to be called his father would be without a son and heir.

Picking up his glass, he took a sip, holding the whisky in his mouth to savour the smoky, peaty flavour, the hint of lime and the salty sharp cleanness.

Ever since birth he'd been surrounded by family. Five hundred years of history flowed through his veins and the progression of his life had had an almost mathematical certainty to it.

But suddenly he'd never felt more alone, more hesitant, more unsure of himself.

And then he'd met Giulietta, and he'd seen a way forward to a shared future with a family that would share his own bloodline.

Closing his eyes, he blew out a breath.

'Is that a good idea?'

His heart kicked against his ribs and, opening his eyes, he glanced across the deck to where his wife was hovering by the bar. She was still wearing the cherry-patterned dress, but she had taken off her make-up and her feet were bare.

So she could run away faster? he thought, his pulse accelerating.

Aware that one wrong word would send her storming back to her cabin, he raised an eyebrow. 'Breathing?' He raised an eyebrow questioningly. 'I suppose that depends on if you'd rather be a widow or a divorcee.'

'I was talking about the whisky.'

As she took a step forward into the light he saw that she wasn't smiling. But she hadn't walked away. He watched her in silence, waiting…

'I'm sorry,' she said quietly. 'For what I said before. About you. I wasn't talking about Carlo not being your father.'

His fingers pressed against the glass. Hearing the truth spoken out loud made it suddenly shockingly real. And yet somehow it was a relief to finally admit even a fragment of his feelings.

He held her gaze. 'It's a bit of a sensitive subject.'

She bit her lip. 'And I'm sorry for not telling you I was still on the pill. I didn't plan to keep taking it,' she said slowly. 'I was going to stop when I came to the end of the cycle. Only then Carlo was ill—' She stopped.

'I remember.'

It had been less than a year after his mother's death. Carlo had been taken to the same hospital where she'd died. For over a week he'd been stricken with fear that he would lose his father too, and torn over whether to tell him the truth.

'Things were difficult.'

Looking back, he knew that he'd been distracted, distant—not just emotionally, but physically, in that he'd often stayed overnight at the hospital in case…

His throat tightened.

But he hadn't just been worried about Carlo. The thought of losing his father had made his plan to start a family of his own seem even more important—urgent, in fact. He hadn't meant it to, but it had taken over everything.

'It's been a long day.' Tilting his head back, he kept his voice steady and walked over to the bar. 'Why don't you join me?'

He had meant it innocently enough but, looking over at her, he saw that his remark had backfired.

'So that's it, is it?' she asked. 'We're just going to sit down and hit the bottle? I thought you wanted to talk.'

Her hands were clenched at her sides, and her glorious eyes were flashing with poorly concealed irritation.

'I mean, that *is* why you dragged me here in the first place, so I would have thought the least you could do is not walk off in the middle of a conversation,' she said hotly.

'Really? I could have sworn you said we were at the end of everything,' he said slowly.

'Don't get smart with me, Ralph.'

Her chin was jutting forward, and with her bare feet and her clenched fists she reminded him again of that cat he'd pulled from the storm drain. His finger brushed against the puckered skin where it had bitten him. What little patience he'd started the day with had almost completely gone.

'Oh, I'm not smart, *bella*. If I were I wouldn't have been hoodwinked by you into thinking you wanted a baby.'

He heard her breath hitch.

'I did want a baby. But babies aren't just an accessory.' Her eyes darted to his wrist. 'They're not some expensive watch. They're tiny little humans with feelings. They need love and security.'

'Are you seriously suggesting I wouldn't love my child?'

She raised her chin. '*Our* child, Ralph. Not yours—ours.' Her gaze locked with his. 'But I don't count, do I? That's the bottom line here.'

The gentle slap of the waves against the boat's hull filled the sudden silence on deck. Far out at sea, the sun was slipping beneath the horizon, the daylight transmuting into darkness.

'You're being foolish.'

She was impossible. Stubborn. Difficult. And scared.

A thought jolted him.

Just like his mother had been.

His shoulders tensed. He'd read those letters and he knew how trapped Francesca had felt in the first few months of her marriage to Carlo. Like Giulietta, she had fled. But not from the country. Instead she had sought comfort in the bed of Niccolò Farnese.

The idea that history might repeat itself—that he might drive his wife into the arms of another man—filled him with a fear and anger he found difficult to control. Anger with her, but mostly with himself.

He'd been a fool not to follow her to England.

A muscle bunched in his jaw. This time he wouldn't let her escape.

She took a step towards him, her hair spilling over her shoulders. 'No, this is foolish. Us trying to make our marriage work.'

His eyes clashed with hers. 'Our marriage worked just fine until you started making false accusations.'

'How can you say that? Our marriage was in pieces.

That's why I thought you were having an affair.' She breathed out shakily. 'You were never there. You were either working or on this bloody boat.'

It was true. His father's illness had given him new responsibilities over the family's various charitable foundations, and, of course, he had to look after his aunts and his cousins.

And all the time, at every board meeting or lunch with his aunts, he'd felt a creeping sense of guilt…of being a fraud.

He glanced across the smooth wooden deck. It had only been here, on the *Alighieri*, that he'd felt 'at home'. Here, drifting out at sea, the rootlessness he'd felt on land had seemed to dissipate.

'I found it hard…being in Verona.'

She was staring at him in silence, and he realised that he had spoken out loud.

Juliet felt her breath catch. His words had startled her. Not their meaning, but their directness.

For weeks now they had been butting heads metaphorically. Or rather she had been butting her head against the brick wall of Ralph's refusal to discuss anything.

Looking up at his face now, she felt her heart contract. He looked tense, troubled, his features tight, and she felt some of her anger fade. 'You were upset.'

Doubly upset, she thought with a pang of guilt.

It would have been unbearable for him to see his father so ill, and so soon after his mother's death. And, of course, he'd also been carrying around the burden of when—*whether*—to tell Carlo the truth.

Ralph might seem strong and unbreakable, but she knew that the worst wounds were the ones beneath the surface.

His eyes found hers. 'I should have told you about my father.' He hesitated. 'I was going to, only then I found the pills, and you saw Vittoria with me, and everything got out of hand.'

And she had fled to England.

It was such a mess. All of it. And it was a mess of their own making. Both of them had held back when they should have opened up with each other.

A lump filled her throat. She felt suddenly helpless—the same kind of helpless she had felt as a child, when everything had been beyond her control. When nothing she'd said or done had seemed to make any difference to her situation.

She held her breath, held on to the panic rising in her chest. It was ironic but the only time she'd felt in control of her life had been with Ralph in Rome—before he'd even proposed to her, when they had been nothing more than lovers.

Except that 'nothing more' made it sound ordinary or just adequate, when in fact their being lovers had been the purest state of all.

Her hands felt clammy. And they had ruined it by rushing into marriage.

She turned to him and said, a little breathlessly, 'Has it ever crossed your mind that this can't be fixed?'

He stared at her for a long moment, and then he shook his head. 'We'll get through it,' he said.

'How?' She felt angry tears prickle her eyes. 'How can we get through this? Everything is wrong between us. Nothing works.'

She felt her heart thud against her ribs. He was standing so close she could feel the heat of his skin, see the heat in his gaze.

There was a long, burning silence.

'Not true,' he said softly. His eyes were fixed on her mouth, and they lingered a moment before rising to meet hers.

The sea was smooth, and beneath her bare feet the smooth wooden deck was solid, but suddenly she was fighting to retain her balance.

'Giulietta…'

He spoke her name gently. His hand when he touched her face was even more gentle. She was afraid to move, almost afraid to breathe. But the temptation to move closer, to touch and trace the shape of his beautiful mouth, made her shake inside.

'Giulietta…'

This time when he spoke her name his fingers slid through her hair, moving with a caressing slowness that stalled her heartbeat. His hands were tangling through her hair and he was tilting her head back, slanting his mouth over hers. She felt something unfurl inside her, like a flower opening its petals towards the sun, as she waited for his kiss.

His lips brushed against hers, their warm breath mingled, and then she leaned in closer, her mouth finding his, unable to tear herself away.

'Trust me, *bella*,' he whispered. 'We work.'

She felt his mouth drop to her neck, to the shadowed hollow at the base of her throat. *We.* That word again. Only this time she was honest with herself—could admit that she had come back to Verona not just for the christening but for this.

For him.

For the touch of his hands and the soft press of his lips on hers.

Head spinning, she stared at him. And then she ran her tongue along his lips.

He made a rough sound, half-growl, half-groan, and then, reaching down his hands, cupped her bottom and lifted her in one movement and carried her to the sofa. He laid her down and, lowering his head, took her mouth again.

'Ho voglia di scoparti qui adesso,' he said hoarsely.

She wanted him too and, reaching up, she clasped his face in her hands and pressed a frantic kiss to his mouth, her teeth catching against his lips.

He leaned into her and she felt the hard press of his erection against the softness of her belly. A moan rose in her throat. Sliding her arms over his shoulders, she pulled him closer, arching her spine, pushing her pelvis upwards, squirming against him, trying to ease the ache that was throbbing between her thighs.

He was reaching for the zip of her dress, but she batted his hand away. She didn't want to wait. She wanted it to be just like it had been in Rome that first time, when they had done it standing up against the bedroom door with his body supporting hers.

'I need you now,' she whispered.

Encircling her waist with his arm, he raised her slightly, and her body clenched as he slid his hand beneath her panties and drew them down over her bare legs. She whimpered, and his mouth found hers and he kissed her thoroughly, his tongue pushing deep into her mouth.

And then she was pulling him closer, her nipples brushing against the hard muscles of his chest, fingers tugging at his zip. Pulling him free, she tightened her hand around him and felt his control snap.

Holding her firmly, he thrust inside her, and she cried out in shock and relief as he began to move.

Her eyes closed. Heat was uncurling inside her, faster and faster, in time with his hips, and she was wrapping her legs around him, holding him close, her hands gripping his shoulders, her body convulsing around him as he erupted inside her with hot, liquid force.

CHAPTER SIX

RALPH WOKE WITH a start, his heart racing, muscles stretched taut. Opening his eyes, he stared around the cabin. It was still dark, but there was a silvery opalescence in the air and he guessed that it was not quite dawn.

For a minute or so he steadied himself, willing the panic to recede. Finally, he managed to breathe. He felt as though he'd been fighting, but it was just a dream. The same vivid dream, part nightmare, part panic attack, that had woken him on and off since his mother had told him the truth about his father.

A dream that seemed to be getting more intense, more vivid, more terrifying…

It always started the same way, with him walking into the Palazzo Gioacchino after work. Everything looked normal—except his mother was still alive and he could hear her and Carlo talking in the drawing room.

But when he walked into the room his father was alone, and instead of welcoming him home Carlo said, 'You shouldn't be here. You're not my son.'

His fingers tightened against the sheet, the memory

of the terror and the guilt pressing down on his ribs. So far, so familiar—but then this time in his dream his father had turned into Giulietta, who had shaken her head and said, 'You shouldn't be here. You're not my husband.'

From somewhere outside the sharp cry of a gull cut through his heartbeat and he felt a rush of relief, for even though he knew it was just a dream it had felt paralysingly real.

Beside him, he felt Giulietta shift in her sleep, and his body tensed as she rolled towards him. But as she settled against him he felt some of his tension ease.

It was called 'grounding'. Using something solid and certain to pull yourself back to reality.

And Giulietta was real. He could feel the heat of her body and the steady beat of her heart, her breath against his bare chest.

She was real and she was here with him.

Against her will?

His hands clenched and then he breathed out slowly. On the boat, yes. But in his bed, no.

His groin tightened at the memory of her touch. It had been almost a rerun of that first time in Rome. There had been no time to savour any preliminaries, no slow, teasing exploration. They hadn't even taken off their clothes. It had been raw and urgent and necessary—a consummation of desire. She had wanted him as much as he'd wanted her.

But last night had to be more than just some mechanical satisfying of hunger.

Why else would she have led him back to this cabin? To this bed.

Thinking back to the moment before they'd kissed, he felt his breathing slow.

He had brought her onto the *Alighieri* wanting answers, wanting to punish her for her hypocrisy, for running away, for deceiving him, for wanting to abandon their marriage.

They had already argued twice—once in the car and then again after he'd tossed onto the bed in their cabin. But neither round had ended satisfactorily, and they had been squaring up to one another again, both of them simmering with rage and frustration.

And then she had looked up into his face and he had seen not just her anger, but her fear.

Her confusion.

Her uncertainty.

It had shaken him, for he understood all those feelings.

And somehow, in his understanding, the bitterness and all the *misunderstandings* of their shared history had dissolved, and they had come together as man and wife. Equals in the face of a shared and potent sexual attraction.

They had made love again and again. In the past, perhaps even in that moment, he would have told himself that sex—the one-of-a-kind sort of sex they shared, anyway—was enough. Should be enough to smooth the tensions in their relationship.

He knew now that it wasn't.

Trust was the issue here.

Giulietta's behaviour had surprised and angered him, and there was still a degree of anger beneath the surface. But the spark of his anger had been lit before they even met.

It had started to flicker way back, when his mother had first told him that Carlo was not his father and his place in the world, the person he'd believed himself to be, had vanished.

A pale pinkish-yellow light was filtering into the cabin now and, gazing down at her sleeping face, he felt his jaw tighten.

It was easy to understand the mistakes he'd made.

Betrayed by the past, feeling trapped in a present where he was torn between continuing to live a lie or ruining the lives of those he loved most by telling the truth, he had become fixated on the future. On having a child.

Only by not telling Giulietta the truth he had forfeited her trust and self-sabotaged his right to the baby he craved so badly.

It was all such a mess of lies and half-truths and secrets.

His body tensed.

And he was still holding back.

Understandably. Trust worked both ways.

And, yes, it didn't sit well with him, the part he'd played in making Giulietta think that her only option was to flee. But the fact was she had chosen to abandon him instead of fighting for their marriage.

His chest felt tight. It had been humiliating, trying to

explain her absence to his family and their friends, and the threat of scandal had been the last thing he'd needed.

She moved against him again, her hand splaying out over his stomach, and he felt a kick of desire just below where her fingers lay twitching against his skin. He ached to pull her closer, to caress and kiss her awake.

It was an admission of sorts, her being here. Only he would be a fool to think that last night had resolved anything except a mutual sexual hunger.

She might be back in his bed, but he wanted her back in his life.

For good.

So he needed to work out how to persuade her that last night hadn't just been a one-off sexual encounter but the first step in their reconciliation.

Feeling calmer, he curved his arm around her waist, anchoring her against his body as he drifted back to sleep.

When he woke again, the bed was empty.

Rolling over, he picked up the remote control by the bed and opened the blinds, blinking as daylight flooded the cabin. It was a perfect day. In the flawless blue sky an apricot sun was already warming the air.

He glanced across the rumpled sheets, his pulse out of sync with his breathing. But where was his wife?

His shoulders tensed, and a rush of irritation flared over his skin. Did she really think she could run from this—from him?

His body had sung at her touch, and he knew he had made her feel the same way, but still she seemed bent on denying that fact.

It took him longer than he'd expected to track her down. She wasn't eating breakfast in the sunshine, or relaxing by the pool. Instead, he found her on the top deck.

He stopped in the doorway, his stomach clenching. Giulietta was less than five feet away. She was wearing peach-coloured shorts and a loose vest with a cross-over back. Her hair was in a high ponytail and he could see the gleam of sweat on the lightly tanned skin of her shoulders.

But it was not her hair or her clothes or even her skin that made his breath catch.

It was her pose.

She was on her knees, leaning forward, with her arms stretched straight ahead and her bottom raised as though in supplication or surrender.

He knew it was a perfectly legitimate yoga position, designed to stretch the spine in both directions. But, predictably, it still took his brain less than three seconds to come up with a modified version of the same pose…this time involving him as well.

Pulse quickening, he found his eyes snagged on the cleft of her buttocks, and he struggled silently against the urge to reach and caress her there, as he had done only hours earlier.

He hadn't thought he'd made any noise… But maybe she had the same inbuilt radar as he did when it came to sensing each other's presence, because the muscles in her back and legs suddenly stiffened, like a deer catching the scent of a predator.

There was a stretch of silence as she rolled up her

spine and sat back on her haunches, and then she stood up in one smooth movement and turned to face him.

He stepped out into the light. *'Buongiorno,'* he said softly. 'Or should I say *namaste*?'

The fringe of her dark lashes fluttered as she tilted her head back, her mouth moving into an approximation of a smile. *'Buongiorno* is fine.'

His fingers twitched. Last night he had felt as if she was his again, and it was tempting to reach out and pull her close, take her mouth with his. But, despite the clamour of his pulse, he stayed where he was.

'That pose looked familiar. It was the Melting Heart, wasn't it?'

She nodded slowly but, judging by the wary expression on her face, her heart hadn't been similarly affected by last night's encounter.

'That's one of the names for it. My teacher calls it the *anahatasana*. It's supposed to be good for tension.'

His eyes rested on her set, pale face. In that case, it wasn't working. She looked tense—nervous, even—and he was pretty sure he knew the reason why. It was the same reason she had not stayed in bed and waited for him to wake this morning.

Clearly they needed to talk about last night.

But they were on a boat in the middle of the Adriatic. Here, they were unmoored from the landlocked constraints of time. Surely he could wait a few moments?

Besides, he thought, as the smell of freshly brewed coffee drifted up from somewhere on board, he'd realised he was ravenously hungry.

'I'm guessing you haven't eaten,' he said slowly.

'Why don't you go and shower? Then we can get some breakfast.'

Fifteen minutes later she joined him on deck. She had changed her clothes, and her hair was still damp from the shower, but the wariness of her expression hadn't changed.

Keeping his expression intentionally bland, he waited while she served herself some fruit and muesli. 'Tea or coffee?' he asked.

'Tea, please.'

Leaning forward, he poured out the tea and added milk, his gaze drifting over the toned curves of her shoulders and arms. He liked what she was wearing. The sleeveless white shirt knotted at her waist and the flirty printed skirt reminded him of some Hitchcock heroine—Grace Kelly or Eva Marie Saint, maybe.

Except he couldn't imagine his wife as a cool, glacial blonde. She was too easy to stir to passion. And to anger.

Impulsively he leaned forward and tucked a stray tortoiseshell curl behind her ear. He felt her tense and, watching the flurry of conflicting emotions chase across her face, he felt his own body tighten too.

It was always there, simmering beneath the surface. One touch was all it took to remind both of them. The difference was she was still fighting it.

Lowering his hand, he leaned back in his seat. 'This is all very civilised,' he said softly.

Her eyes flickered up to meet his. 'You know what would be even more civilised? You turning the *Alighieri* round and taking me back to Venice.'

He held her gaze, letting the silence that followed her remark drift into the warm air.

Her lip curled. 'Doesn't it matter to you that I don't want this?'

'To be on the boat?'

'To be with you anywhere,' she snapped.

He let the silence that followed her remark deliberately lengthen. Then, 'In that case, I think now might be a good time to talk about what happened last night.'

Not just last night, Juliet thought, feeling heat feather her cheeks and her throat. They had reached for one another again and again as night had slipped into a new day.

She felt her pulse stumble.

How could she describe what had happened last night? It had been both inevitable and yet miraculous. Like adding potassium to water and standing back to watch it explode.

She didn't remember falling asleep, and when she'd woken she had momentarily thought that the warm pressure of Ralph's body next to hers was just a dream—some kind of hyper-realistic wish-fulfilment fantasy.

But of course it had been all too real.

She stared at him in silence. Even if she had any it was too late for regrets. But how could anyone regret such blissful sensual fulfilment?

Shifting in her seat, she thought back to the moment when she had finally stopped fighting the inevitable. Except that made her sound passive. Made it sound as if he had plundered her against her will like the heroine of some old Regency romance novel, when in fact their desire had been mutual.

She had matched his hunger. Shaking with eagerness, she had kissed him, pulled him hard against her and inside her aching body. It was she who had led him to their cabin.

It had been a fast and urgent no-holds-barred mating. With mouths, hands, reaching unashamedly for one another, bodies responding to an impulse as old as time.

And it had felt so good.

Glancing across the table, she felt her skin twitch as she remembered what lay beneath that pale blue striped knitted polo shirt and those faded linen shorts.

He had felt so good.

Hard where she was soft, his muscles smooth and taut, his skin warm and sleek. And she had wanted all of him. Skin on skin, the unthinkable freedom to taste, to touch, to savour the teasing, the slow foreplay and the swift passion.

Her eyes dropped to the deck. During her five weeks of self-inflicted celibacy she'd thought she was learning to live without him. She'd been wrong.

But it didn't matter how much she craved him, she was going to have to try harder to learn that particular lesson.

Her shoulders tightened as the words she'd thrown at him last night bumped into one another inside her head.

'Everything is wrong between us. Nothing works.'

He had proved his point: on one level they worked perfectly.

But to acknowledge that Ralph had the power to

render her boneless with desire was to prove another point entirely. That sex was both the cure and the cause of their marital problems—an irresistible quick fix for when words failed as a means of communication.

A slow fix too, she thought, her cheeks heating as she remembered what had happened when they'd finally reached the cabin. Kisses had become caresses and their anger had grown formless, transfigured into passion of a different kind that overcame everything.

Last night's encounter was all part of the pattern of behaviour that had characterised their relationship from the start. It was hardly the basis for a good marriage. And as for having a baby—

Her heart jerked to a halt as a new, devastating thought barged to the front of her mind.

Around her, the warm air pulsed like a bass guitar at a rock concert and she gripped the arms of her chair. She felt suddenly breathless, dizzy, and something of what she was feeling must have shown in her face because he started to shake his head.

'Let me guess,' he said slowly. 'You're going to tell me that what happened was a mistake. That it means nothing and that it won't happen again.'

Actually, she wasn't.

A knot of panic was unravelling inside her chest.

So many times in the past she'd questioned how her mother could have made so many mistakes.

Now she knew.

She stared at him, not trusting herself to speak.

But she couldn't lie. Not after everything they had been through these last months. Not about this.

Her eyes found his. 'I'm not on the pill any more,' she said slowly. 'I stopped taking it just before I went back to England…' Her voice trailed away into silence.

She'd been in such a state—upset, angry, both hating him and missing him. When her period had finished it had felt like fate forcing her to choose a future.

Dazedly, she did some calculations in her head. *It might be okay…*

Heart pounding, she did the calculations once more. *Then again, it might not.*

'I'm about twelve days into my cycle.' *Make that thirteen this morning,* she corrected silently.

He was staring at her, his eyes steady, but she could sense his mind working swiftly through the implications of her words.

'You're saying you could be pregnant.'

He put the emphasis on 'could', but she still felt her pulse accelerate.

Yes, that was what she was saying. And, despite her panic, a shot of pure, shimmering happiness, bright as sunshine, more intoxicating than prosecco, flooded her veins.

She nodded. 'I don't know the odds, but it's definitely possible.'

Her heart thudded. She sounded like some clueless teenager. Worse—she sounded like her mother.

A cool spiderweb of shame wound over her skin. She'd spent so many years trying not to be Nancy Jones, smugly believing herself to be smarter, more stable, better… But she was worse. At least her mother had been only a teenager when she'd had unprotected sex and got pregnant.

She was twenty-five.

There was no excuse for behaving so irresponsibly.

But it had been so fast she hadn't been thinking straight. Truthfully, safe sex had been the last thing on her mind. Fast sex, slow sex, urgent sex, tender sex—but not safe sex.

His expression was unreadable. 'Why did you come off the pill?'

'I don't know.' How was she supposed to explain the chaotic, topsy-turvy flow of her thoughts back then? 'I suppose because I didn't think I needed to be on it any more.'

She watched his face harden infinitesimally, her stomach churning. More implied meanings…more unspoken truths.

'And if you are pregnant?'

His Italian accent was stronger now, muddying his vowels and softening his voice, and she felt her body start to hum beneath his steady gaze.

'Then we'll be having a baby—'

Her words stalled. It was still what she wanted, despite everything. Only it terrified her too—the idea that she might have replicated her own haphazard conception.

'You know nothing would make me happier if you were.'

He was staring at her, and his golden eyes were so incredibly gentle that it was all she could do not to cry. It was too easy to remember their shared hope in those few months of their marriage. Only so much had happened...so much had been revealed as fragile and illusory.

'I might not be,' she said quickly.

The silence stretched away from them, across the sparkling blue sea.

'There's only one way to find out for sure.'

Pushing back his seat, he stood up and pulled out his phone. She watched him walk away, nerves twisting in her throat, and then she stood up too. It was impossible to stay sitting. Her heart felt as though it might burst through her chest.

Trying to steady her breathing, she walked across the deck and braced herself against the handrail, her gaze fixed on the rippling jewel-coloured water.

She should never have come back to Verona. Then none of this would be happening.

Her whole body tensed.

Except then she might not be possibly pregnant, and even now, when she was awash with panic, she felt not just love but a yearning for the baby that might already be embedding itself inside her.

Her heartbeat stuttered as she remembered that moment at the christening when Luca had reached for Lucia, wrapping his arms around her and Raffaelle. Around them guests had stood chatting and laughing, and waiters had offered prosecco and canapés, but they'd had everything they needed.

She held her breath, feeling a tug in her belly like a magnet, and on its heels a swift, shameful envy at being untrammelled by doubt.

Her throat burned with tears.

But that was the difference. Lucia and Luca were meant to be together. They did not and never would know what it felt like to have a child with the wrong person. Or to be that child.

And what if she couldn't pull off being a mother?

The thought stabbed at her. She had tried and failed to be a good daughter and wife—why would being a mother be any different?

'That's sorted.'

His mood had shifted like the breeze coming off the water. The softness had faded from his eyes and his voice had the familiar cool authority of a man used to snapping his fingers and getting his own way.

Her fingers tightened against the cool metal. Abruptly, she turned and faced him, her chin jutting out. 'What are you talking about?'

'That was Dr de Masi. I've made an appointment at her clinic. She says she can do a pregnancy test when you come in.' His gaze held hers. 'Apparently you can do one as early as eight days after conception.'

Eight days.

So soon.

Needing to stop the panic rising in her throat, she resorted to anger. 'And that sorts everything out, does it?' She shook her head. 'Either I'm pregnant or I'm not and then life goes on?'

His gaze didn't shift from hers. 'That's not fair,' he said quietly.

It wasn't. But knowing that only made her feel more defensive.

'Yes, it is.' She couldn't stop the bitterness entering her voice. 'I know you, Ralph.'

'Clearly not.' Taking a step towards her, he caught her wrists, eyes locking with hers. 'If you did, you would know that I wasn't for one moment suggesting that life will just "carry on". But we do need to find out if you're pregnant.'

Her heartbeat stumbled. She couldn't fault the simple logic of his statement. Or his motives for contacting Dr de Masi. Monica de Masi was the obstetrician of choice for wealthy Veronese families. She had met her once and liked her.

But something inside her baulked at the idea of her and Ralph going to the clinic. It made it feel as if this was something they'd planned together as a couple, when actually the reverse was true.

'Can't we just get one of those tests you buy at a pharmacy?' she said, tugging free of his grip.

Their eyes met.

'The Clinica Filomena has an excellent reputation,' he said smoothly. 'And if the test is positive then we will have expert care on hand to advise us and answer questions.'

That was true—and again she couldn't fault his logic. But she knew that the real reason Ralph wanted to go to the clinic had nothing to do with expert care and advice.

He didn't trust her to tell him the truth.

Her fingers curled into fists, guilt and regret jabbing at her. She couldn't blame him. Certainly if their positions had been reversed she would have felt and acted the same way.

Only it hurt.

Not just the fact that he felt that way, but the fact that her actions had let distrust and doubt colour what might be the first few hours of their baby's life.

'I don't just want to buy some kit from the pharmacy,' he said quietly. 'I want to do this properly.'

She bit her lip. 'How can we do that? We've just blundered into it.'

Her mind twisted and turned away from the thought of her own careless conception. She knew that the setting had been somewhat shabbier—a bathroom at a raucous house party rather than a floating palace—but the occasion had shared the same reckless mix of sex and stupidity as her encounter with Ralph.

It made her feel sick.

'I was irresponsible and you were ignorant,' she said flatly.

Ralph's face was expressionless, and then a flicker of frustration crossed it. 'That's one way of looking at it,' he said. 'The other is that we wanted each other. Absolutely and unconditionally.' His thumbs bit into her shoulders. 'Do you know how rare that is, Giulietta? How incredible?'

Despite herself, she felt his words reach down deep inside her. Even now her body still sang from his touch. But that kind of passion carried a sting in the tail.

'It's not that rare.' Her mouth trembled. 'My parents felt like that every single time they had sex.'

She was talking too loudly, and too fast, and she wanted to stop but couldn't seem to call a halt. It was as if the words were like oil gushing from an uncapped well.

'It was what kept them together for so many years—even though their relationship was a disaster and they were completely wrong for one another.'

Ralph heard the break in her voice. It matched the one in his heart.

The thought that Giulietta could be carrying a child…their child…almost undid him. It was what he'd wanted for so long—ever since his mother's bombshell confession had cast him adrift.

It had been a double loss. Losing his mother and learning the truth about his father. He'd been numb with grief…eating standing up, barely sleeping.

It had only been after the funeral that he had been able to register the full extent of the damage, and in those terrible, endless, unnumbered days his life had collapsed like a house of cards.

Everything he'd taken for granted—familial bonds, ancestors stretching back five hundred years, a name that not only opened doors but took them off their hinges—all of it had been proved false.

He'd realised that the gleaming palace of his life had been built on the frailest of foundations. On his ignorance of the truth. But the instant that Giulietta had told him she might be pregnant he had felt as if an anchor had dropped to the seabed.

Not to know for certain was killing him.

He glanced over at her face, but she wouldn't meet his eyes.

Only he knew this wasn't just about him. Or even the possibility that she was pregnant.

He could see there was an exhaustion beneath her panic, as though she had been struggling with something for a long time. *Struggling alone.*

The thought jolted him.

He knew very little about her family or her background. So little, in fact, that what she had told him could be summed up in three sentences.

Her parents were separated.

When her mother had struggled to cope she had been placed with foster parents.

She had left home at sixteen and got a live-in job in the kitchen of a country house hotel.

At the time he hadn't given her reticence much thought. He'd been too distracted by his own unravelling family tree. But clearly it was the parts she'd edited out that mattered most.

Keeping his voice even, he said carefully, 'How long did they stay together?'

She hesitated, then shrugged. 'On and off for about ten years.'

Her eyes were still avoiding his. 'A decade is a long time to stay together,' he said quietly. 'Surely there must have been more to their relationship than sex.'

'There was.' Now she looked at him. 'There was anger. And resentment. And endless misunderstandings. But everything started and ended with sex.' She cleared her throat. 'You know, for a long time I thought that was what people meant by "foreplay"—arguing, making accusations, storming off.'

He heard her swallow.

'I wasn't planned. My parents barely knew each other when my mum got pregnant.'

Her shoulders were braced, limbs taut like a sprinter on the starting blocks, and he wanted to reach out and pull her close, smooth the tension from her body. But he didn't want her to run from him again.

'It was a disaster. They should never have been to-gether. They certainly shouldn't have had a child. And I didn't want to be like them... I didn't want us to be like them. Only it's happened anyway.'

The ache in her voice swallowed him whole. For a few half-seconds he thought about the fears he'd kept hidden, and then he stopped thinking and caught her by the shoulders.

Her body tensed and she jerked against his hands, but he held her still. 'None of us get to choose our parents, *bella*. We don't get to choose how or when or where we're conceived.'

She stopped struggling.

'But we can choose how to live our lives—and you and I...we're not like your parents or mine. And we don't have to make a binary choice between fighting and breaking up.'

Watching her eyes widen, he steadied himself, and just for a moment he considered telling her more about his mother's affair.

But he couldn't bring himself to do so.

Instead, he captured her chin and tilted her face up so that she had to meet his gaze. 'We're going to do this our way, Giulietta. And whatever it takes I'll make it work. I promise.'

Her hands clenched. 'It's not that simple, Ralph.'

'Sure it is.' He spoke with a calmness he didn't feel. 'We go to the clinic. You take the test. And—'

'And then what?'

'I don't know,' he said simply. 'I don't have all the answers. But I do know that if you are pregnant then we can't be constantly at war. We need to be able to talk…to have a relationship for the sake of our child.'

He was choosing his words with the care of a violinist tuning his instrument.

'I know we have a lot of unresolved issues. But if I take you back to Verona then we'll have failed at the first hurdle.'

Something shifted in her eyes, like sunlight on water, and she stiffened for a heartbeat. And then he felt her relax just a fraction.

He relaxed a little too then. 'Look, we have a week until you can take the test. Why don't we spend it here?'

'Do you really need to ask that?' Her brown eyes widened and she twitched free of his grip. 'You brought me here against my will.'

He studied her face. Beneath the defiance she looked incredibly fragile. His heart was hammering his ribs. He felt like a diver standing on the edge of a board. It was all or nothing now. *Crunch time.*

'I can't change that. But if it's what you want then we can turn the boat around now. I'd prefer it if you stayed. Only this time, of your own volition.'

Her eyes flared. 'Why? So we can have sex again?'
Sex.

The word reverberated between them and, watching

the pulse in her throat jump out at him, he had to stop himself from closing the gap between them and pressing his mouth against hers.

'That's not going to happen,' she said.

She sounded adamant, but as she spoke she swayed forward slightly, her body momentarily contradicting her words. He stared down at her, seeing his own hunger reflected in her eyes and in the flush of her cheeks, in the shiver running over her skin.

She was fighting for control.

He was too, his body reacting instantly, viscerally, to the quivering tension in the air.

Pulse trembling, he moved towards her, close enough that all it would take was one more step for him to curl his arm around her waist and join his mouth with hers. He wanted to pull her close as he had last night, as he had so many times in the past, but for this to work he needed to take sex out of the equation.

'You can have your own cabin. There'll be a lock on the door.' His body tensed in revolt, but the need to reassure her took priority over his hunger. 'In nine months' time we could be parents, *bella*. Surely we can call a truce and spend eight days together?' he said softly.

There was a pause. Then, 'Okay.'

Her voice was still taut, but her shoulders had relaxed and he felt a flood of relief. It was a long way from *till death us do part*, but they could start with that.

'I'll stay.' Her eyes clashed with his. 'But this doesn't change anything.'

She was right. Nothing had changed.

Whatever that test said, she was still his wife.

And eight days alone on a boat in the middle of the ocean should be plenty long enough to remind her that he was her husband.

CHAPTER SEVEN

SHRUGGING OFF HER ROBE, Juliet kicked off her flip-flops and dropped down onto one of the teak loungers that clustered around the on-deck pool like animals around a watering hole. She knew she could go for a dip, but it was her brain, not her body, that needed occupation, and she had come prepared.

Picking up her book, she flipped it open, tilting the spine back to avoid the glare of the sun. According to the blurb on the cover, it was 'a pulse-pounding thriller' promising 'an escape from reality'. But, glancing down at the first page, she felt a rush of frustration.

It was going to take a lot more than a fast-paced holiday read to match the drama of her own current situation, she thought, gazing away to the sparkling blue waters of the Adriatic. And as for escaping it…

Her mouth twisted. Right now, a lifeboat might be her best option.

It was just over an hour since she had agreed with Ralph that she would stay on the *Alighieri*.

It was only for eight days.

Hardly a lifetime.

But already she was wondering if she had made yet another mistake by agreeing to stay.

Only it would sound so juvenile to insist on going back now, when she was going to have to see him at the clinic anyway.

The clinic.

She felt her pulse stumble and her fingers twitch. But there was no point in reaching for her phone to check the calendar again. The facts hadn't changed.

They'd had unprotected sex yesterday.

And this morning.

More than once.

And at the time in her cycle when the chances of conception were at their greatest.

So, theoretically, she could be pregnant.

But, since it would be at least a week before she could confirm if she was having Ralph's baby, she was just going to have to wait.

Shifting against the cushions, she steadied her breathing. She hated waiting—hated feeling so uncertain about everything. It reminded her of being a child, shuttled between foster homes, her stomach cramping with hunger and a nagging unspecified dread.

She had learned to manage the feeling by living in the moment, and that had worked well for her. After moving out of her last foster parents' home she'd made a life for herself. She'd had friends, a rented flat, and her hobby—blogging about food—had turned into a job she loved.

Only then she'd fallen in love. And suddenly the

past and the future had been all that mattered: Ralph's past, their future...

Just like that, all her doubts and fears had suddenly been unleashed again, so that for weeks—months, even—she'd felt out of depth.

But she'd never felt more confused than she did right now.

Lifting her arm to shade her face, she squinted across the deck at the docile blue sea.

Her head felt like a slot machine. Each time she thought she had a handle on what she was thinking and feeling something else happened and sent her thoughts spinning.

Her heartbeat skipped.

Like earlier.

They had been talking about her parents. Something he had said had caught her off balance and she had ended up unloading about her past.

She shivered in the sunlight. Not everything. Not the whole sordid story. Nobody needed to hear that. Just the part about the rows and the sex and the fact that she had been conceived without thought.

It was the first time she'd shared the ugliness of those years with anyone. Even just thinking about it had always made it seem too real again, so she'd buried the memories in the deepest corner of her mind.

But this morning, with Ralph, the truth had come tumbling out.

Heart hammering against her ribs, she thought back to that moment when he'd caught her arms, his golden eyes joining his hands to hold her captive.

'*None of us get to choose our parents,* bella. *We don't get to choose how or when or where we're conceived.*'

We.

Her shoulders tensed as she remembered how it had angered her at first, him talking about them in the first-person plural when they were, in effect, estranged.

But this time it hadn't angered her.

Instead it had been as if the last few months had never passed. She had wanted to hold and comfort him, had wanted his arms to close around her.

Picturing the defensive expression on his face, she felt a sudden rush of shame burn through her.

It wasn't hard to imagine his feelings—then or now.

To learn that the man who had raised him from birth was not his father would have been huge. Like an A-bomb detonating in his living room. And she should have been there to support him, but he'd been alone.

They had both been alone with their fears—both been caught up in the events of their pasts. Was it any surprise they had each been swamped by doubt and misunderstandings?

She closed the book.

It made her wonder how different things might be now if they had even once tried to face the past together as a couple, rather than separately as two individuals. If he hadn't kept the truth from her, and she had been able to trust him, would it have made a difference?

Hating that the answer to that question might possibly be yes, she blanked her mind and glanced across the deck. The boat was skirting the coastline now, and as her gaze snagged on a cluster of wildflowers cling- ing heroically to the cliffs she felt her pulse dart.

It was one of the many advantages of having your own private yacht. Space, independence, incompa- rable views… And, of course, if you wanted to, you could stake a claim to one of the many beautiful sandy beaches that were only accessible by water. Just like that you'd have your own completely private idyllic retreat, far from the chattering crowds of tourists.

Her heart beat a little faster as she thought back to the first time Ralph had taken her out on the *Alighieri*. They had driven across the country from Rome, picking up the *Alighieri* in Rimini and then drifting up the Adri- atic coast towards Venice in the cool winter sunshine.

Sometimes they'd made it up on deck, but often they'd just stayed in bed, eating, talking, playing cards and making love as the coastline changed from the un- broken stretches of sand to dramatic eroded cliffs.

They'd dropped anchor in the early evening, just south of the resorts of Rimini and Riccione. From the boat, the beach had been just a teasing sliver of gold, like a crescent moon. Up close it had been magical… otherworldly. A tiny scallop-shaped curve of sand over- looking an iridescent sea the colour of an abalone shell.

Beneath a flawless white moon they had swum in the cool aquamarine water, lost in the magic of being completely alone with each other, and then he had rolled her under him on the wet sand, his body covering hers as the foaming waves spilled over them…

There was a shout from the lower deck, a burst of

laughter, and she was back on the *Alighieri* with the sun burning the air.

It wasn't fair.

It wasn't fair that she could recall it all so clearly.

She didn't want or need to be reminded of how it had felt. It was over, gone, lost… *Wasn't it?*

As the question fizzed inside her head a shadow fell over her face and, looking up, she felt her spine tense with an almost audible snap.

Ralph was standing beside the lounger, his phone in his hand, his body edged with sunlight.

She felt her stomach muscles curl as his gaze roamed over the three triangles of her rose-coloured bikini.

'Hi,' he said softly.

The air felt as though it was electrically charged. Suddenly all her senses were burning.

She cleared her throat. 'Hi.'

It was hard to look at him, but impossible to look away from his preposterously photogenic face.

'Luca called. He sent his love. And these.'

As she gazed up at him he nudged one of the other loungers closer to hers and sat down on it, resting one leg on the other with a familiar masculine confidence that made a pulse of heat tick over her skin.

Her fingers bit into the cover of the book.

She couldn't fault his dark blue swim-shorts or accuse him of underdressing. They were perfectly respectable. And yet they seemed deliberately designed to showcase his superb body: the taut chest, broad shoulders, curving biceps. And the skin that tasted as good as it looked.

She felt Ralph's eyes on her face and her heart thudded hard against her ribs as he held out his phone.

'Here. They're from the christening.'

Grateful for a reason to drag her gaze away from his powerful frame, she took the phone.

She knew hearts couldn't melt but, glancing down at the screen, she felt as if hers was turning to liquid.

Slowly she swiped downwards.

People always said the camera didn't lie, and as far as Lucia and Luca were concerned that was true. They both looked radiant with a happiness that shone from within. But, gazing down at a picture of herself, Juliet wondered at her calm expression. She had been so tense all that day, yet there was no sign of the chaos churning beneath her skin.

Bending lower over the phone, she began scrolling down again—and then her fingers scuffed against the screen and a fluttering mass of butterflies rose up inside her stomach.

It was a photo of Ralph. He was holding Raffaelle and his face was serious. Solemn, almost, as if he was taking a private vow.

Her pulse jumped. She'd told herself there was nothing left between them but a physical attraction. Only gazing down at the photo she knew that it was more complicated than just passion and possession.

With a hand that shook a little, she held out the phone. 'He's a good photographer.'

He stared at her steadily. 'Yes, he is.' His eyes flickered over her bikini again. 'I might take a dip in the pool before lunch. Would you care to join me?'

Her skin felt as if it was suddenly on fire. Being half naked on a lounger was one thing. Being half naked in a pool with Ralph in swim-shorts was something else entirely.

She managed a small, taut smile. 'I'll think I'll just read my book.'

There was a short pulsing silence as his eyes flickered over the cover and then he shrugged. 'Okay.'

Heart pounding, she watched as he tossed his phone onto the lounger and stood up. Relief washed over her as he executed a perfect dive into the pool and disappeared beneath the water.

An hour later it was time for lunch.

Forking the delicious antipasti of stuffed peppers, parmigiana and tiny pink prawns into her mouth, she was surprised to find she was really quite hungry. It was her favourite kind of food. Simple ingredients cooked well. But she knew it was more than the food.

It was easy being with him—easier than it should be, she thought. Easier than it had been even a few weeks ago. Easy, too, to see why she had fallen so deeply under his spell.

And might do so again?

She stared down at the cutlery, her eyes tracing the intricate embossed pattern on the handle of her spoon.

All she had to do was say the words. Only she'd felt like this before and been wrong. What if she was wrong again?

As they waited for their plates to be cleared away Ralph lounged back in his seat, tilting his face up to the sun. 'I was chatting to Franco earlier, and he told me about a place just down the coast where we can drop anchor.'

Her heart skipped. Could he read minds? Had that night beneath the stars stuck in his mind too? Or was it just coincidence?

His eyes met hers. 'I thought maybe we might go ashore.'

She held his gaze. 'You're not worried I might run away?'

A faint smile tugged the corners of his mouth. 'Should I be?'

They both knew it was a hypothetical question. She would need crampons to climb the cliffs that hugged the patches of sand edging this stretch of the coast. But she knew that he wanted to gauge her mood. To find out if their truce was holding.

Glancing past him, she focused her attention on the plunging sandstone cliffs. There was a part of her that was relieved to have a respite from fighting him.

She looked up to find him watching her, and suddenly she was conscious of every breath, of the heavy pulse pounding through her body.

He was on the other side of the table, but it felt as if there was no distance between them. She felt hot and tingly, as if his golden gaze had set off firecrackers beneath her skin.

No, Ralph didn't have to worry about her running away—but she should be worried about why she'd stayed.

Forcing herself to hold his gaze, she shook her head. 'Of course not. We made an agreement. I said I'd stay until the appointment with Dr de Masi, and that's what I'm going to do.'

Later, as they sped across the translucent water to the cove Franco had told them about, Ralph replayed her words inside his head, frustration swelling up inside him like the curling bow wave at the front of the dinghy.

She didn't trust him. Still.

But was that such a surprise? It required time to repair and restore trust.

He felt a rush of panic. What if he ran out of time, like his mother had?

His hands clenched. He wanted to scoop Giulietta into his arms as he'd done at the marina. Only this time he didn't want to let go of her.

But everything was so finely balanced at the moment. He didn't want to do anything that might risk them going backwards.

The cove was deserted—and beautiful. Powder-soft ivory-coloured sand, clear shallow water and the occasional piece of bleached driftwood.

He had hoped she might swim with him, but instead she lay down on the comfortable oversized cushions the crew had brought over earlier and began reading her book.

The water was perfect and, closing off his mind, he swam until his muscles ached.

Finally he'd had enough, and he made his way up the beach, his eyes fixed on his wife. She'd changed position. Now she was sitting with one arm curled around her knees, her tawny hair framing her face.

He felt his heart contract. She looked so young, and yet there was a tension to her shoulders as if she was carrying the weight of the world.

When he dropped down beside her she didn't look up from her book and, rolling onto his side, he sighed. 'I've got to say, this isn't doing much for my ego.'

There was a pause and then she lifted her face, frowning. 'What do you mean?'

'I'm not used to playing second fiddle—particularly to a book. Must be a real page-turner,' he prompted, sitting up.

There was another pause, and then she shrugged. 'Actually, I haven't managed to get past the first chapter.'

He raised an eyebrow. 'Really?' Ducking his head, he tipped the cover towards him. 'It says here it's "gripping, pacy, and utterly addictive".'

He watched the corners of her mouth lift.

'It probably is. I just can't concentrate.'

'Why not?

'I've got a lot on my mind.'

'So what's bothering you?' He screwed up his face. 'I mean, other than being abducted and possibly getting pregnant by a man you want to divorce.'

They stared at one another in silence, and then she smiled, and suddenly he was smiling too.

Then her mouth started to tremble. 'You make it so hard for me to fight you,' she said shakily.

The sheen of tears in her eyes made his body tense

in shock. He'd never seen his wife cry. And he hated it that he had been the one to change that fact.

'That's because I don't want to fight with you any more, *bella*.' He kept his voice deliberately steady. 'I want to start again. Go back to the beginning.'

The beginning: Rome.

Memories of those first few days together moved smoothly inside his head like the picture strip in a spinning zoetrope.

It had been perfect.

Heat and passion.

Skin on skin.

And an all-encompassing need.

They might have met in Rome, but he didn't need to be in Verona to know that she was the one, his Giulietta. In that moment it was as if he could see the rest of his life with her at the centre. Only, through arrogance and stupidity, he had not just let her go, he had driven her from their home.

'Do you think we could do that, Giulietta? Do you think we could start over?'

His heart stumbled when she started shaking her head. 'I don't know if we can. I don't know if *I* can…'

Something in her voice reminded him of their conversation earlier, when she'd told him about her parents and their rows and their making up. There had been the same note of fatigue—defeat, even—and he felt suddenly out of his depth. He hadn't even managed to sort out his own problems. Why did he think he could help soothe her pain?

Because you're her husband, he told himself fiercely. *That's why.*

He took a breath. 'When did you last see them?' he said quietly. 'Your parents?'

She was silent for so long he thought he'd lost her, but then he realised she was searching for something to say that would be enough but not too much.

He knew that feeling well.

'I don't know,' she said finally. 'My dad was never really there. He was always coming and going. Mostly going.' Her lips twisted. 'I suppose I was probably about nine when he stopped coming back.'

She glanced past him, looking upwards, her eyes tracking the contrails of a plane across the sky.

'I don't remember the exact day, but it was October and it was foggy. He went out for bread and never came back.' Despite the heat of the sun, she sounded shivery. 'It was like the fog just swallowed him up...' Her words drifted into silence.

'And your mum?'

Now her eyes clashed with his, the brown dark and defensive.

'Why are you asking all these questions?' She had scooted away from him and she was holding the book in front of her chest like a shield.

'Because you're my wife,' he said quietly, reaching over and capturing her hand. 'And because I should have asked you when we first met.'

It hurt, admitting that to himself—to her. But at the time her past, her background, had been secondary to his. Or rather secondary to the earth-shattering repercussions of finding out that everything he had taken for granted was a lie.

He'd arrogantly assumed that nothing in her ordinary little life could be as devastating as finding out he wasn't a Castellucci.

He felt a rush of self-loathing. He'd had so much in his life, an excess of everything—*even fathers*—and yet he had failed to give his wife the reassurance and support she needed.

Across the beach, the waves were tumbling onto the sand, each one washing away the lacy patterns of the last. If only he could so easily erase the mistakes he'd made.

But, then again, maybe this shouldn't be easy.

Clearly she thought so too.

She pulled her hand free. Her mouth was trembling. 'But you didn't.'

'No, I didn't.' He pushed back against the regret. 'And that's on me. I let you down, and I hurt you. And I know I can't change what I did, but I will do everything in my power to earn your trust back.'

He could see the conflict in her eyes, the longing to believe his words vying with the hurt, and he hated it that he had so carelessly lost her trust.

She breathed out shakily. 'This isn't all on you. I was wrong too. I wouldn't have told you anything even if you had asked me about my parents. I didn't want you to know about them…about me.' Her voice was trembling now. 'Talking about it is so hard. It makes it all feel real again.'

He reached out and caught her hand again. 'Makes what feel real?' he asked gently.

'How it felt, living like that.'

This time, her fingers tightened around his.

'It wasn't just the rows. They were alcoholics. If they weren't out getting wasted, they were hungover and hopeless. When my dad left for good, my mum just gave up. One day she took some pills—'

The words sounded stark, ugly against the soft beauty of the beach. And there was a seam of pain in her voice now that made his stomach twist with rage. She had been nine years old…just a little girl.

'What happened?'

'I tried to dig them out of her mouth but she wouldn't wake up. So I called an ambulance. She was okay, but there was no one to look after me so I went to stay with Rebecca and Tim.'

She was curled over now, her shoulders hunched, as if she was surrounded by a pack of wolves. Maybe she felt that way.

'They were my first foster parents.'

First. For such a small word it packed a hell of a punch.

He stared at her small, tense body, his heart aching with emotions that felt too big to be contained. 'But there were others?'

She nodded. 'Lots of people like me…they just slip through the net. So I was lucky, really.'

He watched her fingers bunch into a fist. The gesture made his whole body hurt.

'I suppose it was just not knowing each time if there

would be anyone there to catch me that was so terrible…'

His ribs ached.

For her, love had proved dangerous. What should have been solid—the love of her parents—had been consistently weak and unreliable, and yet she had not given up. Despite all those betrayals of her childhood she had let herself feel again, let herself love him.

Unlike him, she had faced her fears, her doubts, head-on, trusting to love, *trusting him*.

'What about now? Do you have anything to do with her?'

She cleared her throat. 'Not since I was sixteen. That's when we last spoke. She texts me sometimes, but I made the decision to cut her out of my life.'

She was looking at him, but not quite meeting his eyes.

'I know she's my mum, but being around her makes me feel so out of control, so powerless, and it scares me…'

Her voice wavered, and he had closed the gap between them and pulled her into his arms before he'd even realised what he was doing.

A sob caught in her throat and she crumpled against him. He held her tightly, stroking her silken hair and telling her over and over again that everything would be all right, swapping back and forth from English to Italian until finally she was calm.

'That's why you went back to England,' he said hoarsely. 'I'd made you feel powerless.'

He felt her shiver.

'I panicked. I thought it was something in me—something I was doing—and that was why you wanted someone else.'

Cupping her chin, he tipped her face up to his, fearing and knowing that he hadn't made his feelings for her sufficiently clear. 'I didn't want anyone else. I never have. I want you—all and every possible version of you.'

He felt her hands flutter against his chest and, looking down, felt heat flood his veins. Her eyes were wide and soft, her body pressing against his was softer still, and he was on the verge of kissing her.

But something held him back. The need to demonstrate that he wanted her for more than just sex. That he *needed* to be there for her.

And he needed her to be there for him.

His stomach clenched.

Could he tell her? Could he share his fears?

The dark, clammy panic rose inside him like an intruder, pinning him down and suffocating him. Heart swelling, he glanced down at her tear-stained face. Another time, maybe. This was about her, and her needs, not his, and she needed to know that she was deserving of love—his love.

'You don't need to be scared any more, *bella*. I'll always be there to catch you. Always.' Leaning down, he kissed her on the forehead, his hand moving over her cheek. 'I think we should get back to the boat now.'

Away from this secluded little beach, where he might be tempted to give in to lust or, worse, to the need to unburden the misery in his heart.

* * *

Stepping out of the shower, Juliet tucked the plush towel around her body, knotting it above her breasts. It wasn't late—not much past nine—but after a light supper she had retreated to her cabin, claiming tiredness.

And it was true. She felt exhausted and dazed. Just as if she'd just finished a race she had been training for all her life.

For so long she had dreaded talking about her childhood—had spent years avoiding the subject or telling a carefully edited version of her past. And yet she'd done it. She'd told Ralph the truth. And, although it had been distressing having to remember it all, it had been easier than she'd expected.

He'd made it easy for her.

Her heart bumped against her ribs.

She still couldn't quite believe everything that had happened since she'd returned to Verona. So much had changed in such a short time.

They had changed.

Take today. They had fought—*again*—but the difference was that this time they had finished the conversation. And they hadn't ended up having sex.

No thanks to her.

Remembering the moment when he'd told her he wanted her, she felt her skin grow suddenly warm.

Pressed against his beautiful bare chest, she had felt so weak in the face of her need for him that she had been seconds away from pulling his head down to hers and forgetting about the consequences.

Again.

Without thinking she moved her hand to her stomach, to the possible consequences of the last time she'd given in to just such an urge.

Her fingers trembled against the towel.

She might not be pregnant, but the possibility had broken the impasse between them. It had shown both of them that although they might be flawed, change was not just possible but in their hands.

Their hands.

His hands.

She felt her body tense and soften at the same time. He had the most instinctive sense of touch, reading her body like a healer. Only it wasn't her body she was talking about. He had helped heal the scars on her soul.

She felt calmer. But it was more than that. It was as though someone had shifted a burden from her shoulders so that she no longer felt like that unloved—worse, unlovable—little girl.

Her throat was suddenly so tight it was hard to breathe.

Not someone.

Ralph.

Pulse pounding, she walked over to the connecting door between their cabins and gently pushed it open.

Ralph was standing by the bed. He too was naked, except for the towel wrapped around his waist. He was rubbing his hair with another towel.

Glancing over at her, his face tensed. 'Giulietta—is something wrong?'

Dropping the towel, he crossed the cabin in two long strides.

'No. I…'

As her eyes slid over the powerful muscles of his chest she was momentarily lost for words. His body was just so perfect.

'Did you want to talk to me?' He was looking down at her, his beautiful golden eyes trained on her face.

She blinked, tried to refocus her brain. But she couldn't seem to think straight. Only why did she need to think at all? No thought was required for what she wanted—and she did want him, with an intensity and a freedom she had never felt before. Not even in Rome.

Then she had been…

Her heart was pounding so hard she thought it might burst. Taking a step forward, she leaned into him, her hands reaching up to capture his face. Tilting her head slightly, she brushed her lips against his.

'Kiss me.'

As she breathed the words into his mouth she felt him tense for a fraction of a second, and then his hands were sliding beneath the towel, fingers splaying against her back, his lips so warm and urgent that she felt a pit of need open up inside her.

Parting her lips, he kissed her more deeply, and then he pulled her closer, close enough that she could feel the thick outline of his erection pushing against her stomach.

She felt her breath tangle as he lifted her hair from her shoulder, tugging it sideways to expose the curve of her throat. And then he was licking her skin, running his tongue along her clavicle to the pulse leaping beneath the skin.

'*La tua pelle sembra sete,*' he said hoarsely. His eyes found hers, the pupils huge and shockingly dark against the gold of the iris. 'You want this.'

It was a statement of fact.

Licking her lips, she nodded slowly. 'Yes.'

He groaned as she began moving against him. '*Mi vuoi...*'

She shivered inside. Her body was tense. Hot. Damp. Her breasts felt heavy. She ached for his touch.

'*Si,*' she said softly, her hands reaching down to where the towel hugged his abs. '*Ti voglio così tanto.*'

CHAPTER EIGHT

HOOKING HER FINGERS beneath the damp fabric, she tugged gently, her pulse jumping in her throat as the towel slid to the floor. Now he was naked too. Naked and aroused. *Very* aroused.

'My turn,' he whispered softly.

Her mouth went dry as he reached out and pulled at the knot between her breasts. His face stilled, and she felt her muscles clench as he reached out to caress first her cheek and the curve of jaw, then lower to her taut ruched nipples.

She moaned softly as his fingers teased first one then the other. Her body tightened with need. She was so hot and hungry for him.

Her hand twitched against his skin. He was looking down at her in silence, his eyes like molten gold. 'You like that?' he said softly.

She nodded slowly, feeling an answering wetness between her thighs as he gently cupped her breasts in his hands and kissed her slowly and deeply.

Breathing out raggedly, she reached down and wrapped her hand around his hard length, a sharp heat shooting through her as he grunted against her mouth. Head swimming, she caressed the velvet-smooth skin, feeling him pulse in her hand.

'You're killing me, baby,' he groaned.

Batting her hand away, he lifted her up and lowered her onto the bed.

Gazing down at her, Ralph felt as though his skin was going to catch fire. She was so beautiful, and she was his to explore, to pleasure.

Leaning forward, he drew first one and then the other taut nipple into his mouth, his body tensing as the blunt head of his erection brushed against where she was already so wet for him.

He touched her lightly between her thighs. She felt slick and white-hot. Shaking with need, he ran his hands over her body as she arched upwards to meet his touch. For a moment he admired the smooth, flawless skin, the small breasts and the curve of her belly, and then, lowering his face, he kissed a path from her stomach to the triangle of fine dark hair.

Her fingers tightened on his head. She was moving restlessly, squirming against his mouth, and he slid his hand beneath the curve of her buttocks, lifting her up. He could feel tiny shivers of anticipation darting across her skin as he stroked her trembling thighs with his thumbs, inhaling her salty damp scent.

She was already swollen and, flattening his tongue, he began licking her clitoris with slow, precise strokes, again and again, until he was no longer conscious of anything but the pulse beating against his tongue and her soft moans.

Suddenly her hands jerked. 'No, not like this.' She was panting. 'I want you inside me.' Her eyes flared. 'You need a—'

'I'll get a condom.' His voice was husky.

They'd both spoken at once.

He rolled off the bed and Juliet watched dazedly, her breath trapped in her throat, as he tore open the foil. The need to touch, to taste, overwhelmed her and, cupping him in her hand, she leaned forward, flicking her tongue over the smooth polished head.

He made a rough sound in the back of his throat. Gripping her hair, he let her take him into her mouth, and then she felt him jerk away and he grabbed her wrist.

'Next time.'

With fingers that shook slightly he rolled the condom on, and then, dropping down on the bed, he pulled her onto his lap. She kissed him hungrily, nipping his lips with her teeth, and then he was holding her hips, raising her up, guiding himself into her body. His groan mixed with her gasp of pleasure as he slid into her.

Pulse hammering, she felt Ralph grip her waist, clamping her body to his as she started to roll back and forth.

Threading his fingers through her hair, he tipped back her head, baring her throat to his tongue and his lips. His hand moved to her clitoris, working in time with her frantically arching pelvis.

Juliet felt her pulse soar. 'Yes…' She moaned the word against his mouth, turning it from one syllable to five. Her skin was so hot and tight—but not as tight as she felt on the inside.

His thumb was pushing her to the edge, the fluttering ache between her legs was now impossible to ignore, and she shuddered helplessly, muscles rippling, her body gripping him, becoming his.

And then she cried out as he tensed, slamming into her, and there was nothing that mattered except Ralph and the power of his hard body driving into hers.

The shout filled her head and, jolted from sleep, Juliet struggled onto her side. The last thing she could remember was Ralph burying his face in her hair, his arms curving around her, anchoring her to his body as her heartbeat slowed.

Now her heart was hammering inside her ribcage.

She reached out.

In the darkness beside her Ralph was shuddering, his arms pushing against the covers.

'Ralph!'

She felt him tense as her voice echoed sharply round the silent cabin and, reaching out again, she fumbled for the light.

By the time she turned round he was sitting on the edge of the bed, his head in his hands.

'Ralph,' she said again, more softly this time. 'It's okay. You were having a nightmare but it's over now.'

He flinched as she touched his shoulder. His skin felt warm, but he was shivering as if he had a fever.

She stared down at him uncertainly. Ralph had always been a bad sleeper. But this didn't seem like the aftermath of a nightmare. He seemed barely aware of her presence and his breathing sounded jerky.

Sliding onto the floor, she knelt in front of him. 'You're going to be fine.'

Gently she reached up and took his hands in hers. He didn't reply, but she felt his fingers tighten around hers.

'It's okay, I'm not going anywhere. I'm going to stay right here,' she said quietly.

He still hadn't spoken, but he hadn't let go of her hands either and so, keeping her voice calm and fluid, she carried on talking.

She talked about the food they had shared that evening, and the pictures Luca had sent of the christening, until finally she felt his breathing grow steadier.

'Would you like a glass of water?' she asked.

For a moment she didn't think he would respond, but then he nodded.

'Wait a second,' she whispered.

Standing up, she went to the bathroom and filled a glass with water from the tap.

'Here.' She handed him the glass.

He took it without looking up. 'Thank you.'

His voice sounded frayed, as if he had torn it by shouting, and she felt a sudden rage at whatever it was that had crept into his dreams.

'How are you feeling now?' She sat down beside him, keeping her movements small and her voice steady.

'Better.'

She watched as he ran a hand over his face.

'I'm sorry,' he said quietly.

'For what?' She hesitated a moment, then took his hand again.

'For waking you up like that. I didn't hurt you, did I?' Now he looked at her, his eyes desperately searching her face.

'No, of course you didn't hurt me.'

'I could have done. I didn't know what I was doing.' He sounded distraught.

'You didn't do anything. You were just moving about and then you shouted something—'

But he was shaking his head. 'I'll sleep next door.'

He made as if to stand up, but she caught his arm.

'No, Ralph. You're not sleeping next door. If you do, then I'm coming with you.'

He stiffened, but didn't resist as she tugged him gently down onto the bed. His body was still trembling and, reaching round him, she grabbed a sweatshirt from the chair by the bed.

'Here—put this on.'

She watched as he pulled it over his head, breathing shakily into the silence of the cabin.

'It might help...' She hesitated, catching sight of the shuttered expression on his face, then tried again. 'It might help to talk about it.'

Her words hung in the air.

He glanced over at her and shook his head, then looked down at his hands. 'There's no need. It was just a nightmare...a bad dream. You said so yourself.'

She felt her heart beat faster.

Ever since she'd known him Ralph had slept badly,

shifting restlessly and often waking in the night. The only exception to that pattern had been during those first few weeks in Rome—but of course then he had been on holiday.

This was different.

He had seemed disorientated, almost unaware of her and his surroundings. And scared. As if the nightmare hadn't stopped when he'd woken up.

She knew that feeling well.

'Is that what you think it was? Just a bad dream?'

Her question was level-toned, but she felt him go still. The silence echoed round the cabin.

Normally at this point he would either kiss her until she couldn't remember having asked the question, or give her one of those cool, enigmatic smiles that meant he was about to change the subject.

But this time he kept staring down at his hands. 'I don't know.'

She could hear the heaviness, the despair in his voice.

'I don't know,' he said again. 'I think it starts out as a bad dream.'

Starts.

So it wasn't a one-off.

'And then what happens?' she asked, and gazed away, giving him time.

The cabin was silent for a moment, and then he shrugged.

'I wake up and there's this weight crushing my chest.' He pressed a clenched hand against his breastbone. 'It feels as if something is sitting on me—like in that painting.'

'*The Nightmare*,' she said quietly.

Like most people, she knew the Fuseli painting. The image of a beautiful sleeping woman draped across a bed with a hunched creature with the face of a gargoyle crouching on her stomach was enough to give anyone nightmares.

She felt him shudder and, reaching out, prised his fingers apart and took his hand in hers again.

'I try to push it off me, but I can't, and then I realise I'm still asleep, and that I'm never going to wake up.'

It sounded terrifying. Doubly terrifying for an intensely physical man like Ralph.

She glanced down at the sculpted muscles of his thighs. He might be a billionaire businessman, with a highly trained security team tracking his every movement, but Ralph could take care of himself. Not only did he work out regularly, but he had been trained in the Russian martial art Systema.

'But you do wake up?' she said gently.

He nodded slowly. 'But I can't breathe. It's like I'm choking. The first time it happened I thought I was having a heart attack.'

It obviously hadn't been a heart attack, but it hadn't been just a bad dream either.

'Oh, Ralph…' As she whispered his name he turned to look at her, a muscle flickering in his jaw, and she felt her own heart twist.

'I thought it would stop.'

His eyes looked desperate and she nodded quickly.

'It will.' They were the only words she could force past the lump in her throat. 'But panic attacks don't go away on their own. There's usually a trigger.' She hesitated. 'What's the dream that starts it about? Or can't you remember?'

The sudden tension in his body told her that she was on the right track.

'I can remember it,' he said flatly.

There was a long silence, and then he inhaled sharply.

'It's always the same. I come home after work and everything seems normal, only my mother is still alive, and I can hear her and my father talking.'

Her throat was tight. No matter how bad her own pain had been, nothing could compete with hearing his…feeling his. It felt like a vice around her heart.

'I walk into the drawing room, but my father is alone, and he turns to me and he says, "You shouldn't be here. You're not my son. You'll never be my son."'

He ran his hand over his face, and with a shock she realised that he was close to tears.

'You *are* his son,' she said fiercely. 'You've been his son for thirty years. His face lights up when you walk into the room. He loves you so much.'

'And I love him.' His voice was rough. 'And I don't want to keep lying to him. But I don't want to hurt him either.' He looked exhausted all of a sudden. 'He's already lost his wife. If I tell him the truth it'll be like losing her all over again.' A tremor started in his hands. 'If I tell him the truth he'll lose his son and heir too. He'll be the last of the Castelluccis.'

There was a long, dull silence. Juliet felt her pulse accelerate. She hadn't really registered the wider implications before, but Ralph was right. Without him, the Castellucci name would disappear.

Gazing over at his taut profile, she felt her heart twist. It must have been hard enough finding out his mother had been unfaithful and his father was not his father, but this was bigger than Ralph.

What he chose to do would have an impact on his entire family.

No wonder Francesca had held her secret close for so long. And yet something had pushed her to confess the truth...

'What did your mother want you to do?' she asked carefully. 'I know she couldn't bear to tell Carlo herself, but surely she wouldn't have told you if she didn't want him to know eventually.'

There was another silence, this one longer.

Then, 'She didn't want to tell me.' He met her eyes and his mouth twisted. 'Vittoria told me. She found some letters my mother wrote to her father, Niccolò, and she came to the house. She was so upset, making all kinds of accusations... Luckily I was there on my own.'

His hand clenched painfully around hers.

Luckily in some ways, she thought. But it would have been better for Ralph if Francesca and Carlo had been there. Then he would have been spared all these months of carrying the burden of guilt and uncertainty.

'Did you look at the letters?' she asked.

His beautiful mouth curved into a grimace. 'Yes. I don't know why. Maybe I shouldn't have. I suppose I wanted to prove her wrong, but I recognised her handwriting and it was clear that they'd been having an affair.'

He was silent again.

Gazing up at the smooth planes of his face, Juliet tried to imagine what it must have felt like to read those letters. The shock, the pain of betrayal, the burden of knowledge…

'Is that when you talked to your mother?' she said quietly.

He shook his head. 'That was the day they got her test results back from the hospital. They were both stunned…devastated… I couldn't—' Tears pricked the back of her eyes and he breathed out unsteadily.

She tightened her grip on his hand. 'Of course you couldn't. No one could.'

He was looking down at his hand in hers, his eyes locked on the signet ring on his little finger. 'Sometimes I think I should have just left it alone. Kept what Vittoria told me to myself. Only I couldn't. I think I knew that there was more to it.'

Juliet stared at him in silence. It was easy now to understand why he had found it so hard to confront the problems in their marriage. Look at what had happened last time he'd tried: his whole world had come tumbling down.

Her throat was tight and aching. It ached for him.

'What did she say when you did talk to her?' she asked.

'Nothing. She wouldn't talk about it.' There was a heaviness in his voice now, a note of finality. 'Not until the end. That's when she told me that Carlo wasn't my biological father.'

He looked up at Juliet and she saw his eyes were full of unshed tears.

'I knew that anyway by then. I'd taken a DNA test. I just wanted her to say it to my face, so I could remember her telling me the truth.'

'And she did tell you the truth.' She spoke firmly, her hand tightening on his.

It felt like it had in Rome, when they had been so in tune with one another—only then it had been physical. This time he had stripped off more than just his clothes. He had bared his soul.

'She told you everything. The whole truth. Not just that she had an affair. But that Carlo wasn't your father. She didn't have to do that, but she did. Because she wanted you to have the choice. The choice she took from you before you were born.'

'But I don't want to choose.' His mouth twisted. 'I just want to do what's right.'

'You're already doing that,' she said slowly. 'You run your business. You take care of your family, your father—'

'I didn't take care of you.' The pain was there again, at the edges of his voice. 'I hurt you so badly you ran away.'

'We hurt each other—and I came back.'

His eyes found hers. 'For the christening.'

She held his gaze. 'For that too.' Reaching up, she cupped his face. 'Whatever you choose to do will be the right thing.'

She could feel his pain so acutely that it made her own eyes fill with tears, and without thinking she slid both arms around him and pulled him close.

He breathed out shakily. 'I miss her so much… I don't want to lose him as well.'

Light was starting to squeeze around the blinds and, her heart pounding, she took a breath. 'You can't lose him, Ralph. Carlo raised you, and he loves you, and no test can change that.' She forced a smile. 'DNA makes a baby, not a father. Trust me—I know.'

He pulled her closer, holding her tightly. 'You deserved so much better. You *deserve* so much better than this…than me.'

She could feel his heart beating in time with hers.

'I'm sorry…' He struggled with the words, a muscle working in his jaw. 'I'm sorry you had to see me like this.'

Pulling away slightly, she looked up at him. 'You're my husband. We took vows, remember? I know bad dreams and panic attacks aren't mentioned specifically, but I reckon they're covered by "in sickness and in health" or maybe "for better or worse".'

He looked up at her in silence, and her heart performed a perfect somersault as she felt the full impact of his beautiful golden eyes.

'What?' She frowned. 'What is it?'

He slid his hands into her hair and tilted her face up to his. 'That's the first time you've acknowledged that I'm your husband since you got back from England,' he said softly.

Watching her face, Ralph held his breath. There was a silence. Their eyes met.

She blinked, then looked down. 'I suppose it is.'

The cabin fell silent.

'So, I was wondering,' he said slowly, 'and hoping that maybe you might have changed your mind…'

As she looked up at him the glow from the bedside lamp lit up her face, emphasising both its softness and its strength.

'About getting a divorce. You see, I meant what I said on the beach about us trying again.' Reaching out, he touched her stomach gently. 'I want to spend the rest of my life with you. Have children with you. Grow old with you. Do you think we could do that, *bella*? Do you think we could try again?'

She held his gaze, and then slowly she nodded. 'Yes, I think we could.'

Her words—so simple, so honest—made his heart turn over and emotion shudder through his body. He leaned in to kiss her, sliding his tongue over her lips and then into her mouth.

Her hands slid over his stomach, and he sucked in a breath and then tugged the sweatshirt over his head and reached for her…

When he woke, the sun was already high in the cloudless blue sky.

Giulietta was still asleep.

He stared down at her, holding his breath.

Her hair was a dark, swirling storm cloud on the pillow, and with her eyelashes feathering the curve of her cheekbone she looked exactly like an illustration in a book of fairy tales. A beautiful sleeping princess, trapped in a tower, waiting to be rescued by her prince.

His chest tightened.

Except that last night it had been he who had needed rescuing. He had been the one drowning in panic, and Giulietta had chased away his demons.

He dressed noiselessly and, resisting the urge to wake her with a kiss, made his way out onto the private deck beside their cabin.

It was another beautiful day, but as he walked into the sunlight he felt a rush of emotion that had nothing to do with the warm air or the sea or the sky. It was as if he had woken not just from a long sleep but from a living nightmare. He felt calmer than he had in months.

And it was all down to Giulietta.

His fingers tightened against the handrail.

Up until a few hours ago he'd barely been able to acknowledge the breathless, heart-hammering episodes that had been plaguing his nights, much less give them a name. But Juliet had done both. And more. She had agreed to give their marriage a second chance.

'Ralph…'

He turned, his heart missing a beat.

Juliet was standing in the doorway. Her hair was spilling over her shoulders in untidy curls and she was wearing the T-shirt he'd been wearing yesterday.

'Why didn't you wake me?' she said huskily.

Glancing down at her bare legs and imagining them wrapped around his waist, he felt his body harden.

Good question.

'I thought you needed to sleep.'

'Did *you* sleep?'

Hearing the concern in her voice, he felt his heart

contract. 'Yes, I did.' He took a step towards her and pulled her against him. 'Thanks to you.'

He kissed her gently on the mouth, the tip of his tongue parting her lips briefly, and the hitch of her breath made him feel vertiginous with equal parts of hunger and relief.

'What was that for?' she asked.

'Lots of different things,' he said softly. 'Looking better in my T-shirt than I do.' Leaning forward, he kissed her again. 'Looking after me last night. And for agreeing to give us—*me*—a second chance.'

His words brought her eyes back to his. Gazing down at her face, he tightened his hands around her waist, his emotions almost too raw to contain so that he was suddenly afraid he might weep.

How could he have let it happen? That distance between them? He had come so close to losing her. To losing the one person who saw beneath the perfect façade...the one woman who knew him completely, inside and out.

And he knew her. He understood her now. He knew about the lonely little girl who had been raised by strangers and he understood her mistrust and her self-doubt.

That she had survived was miraculous.

Only she hadn't just survived. She had triumphed. And he was in awe of her strength, her determination, her courage.

There was nothing he wouldn't do for her, but mostly he wanted to hold her close, to wrap his body around hers.

Suddenly he was struggling to fill his lungs with

air. He was so hungry for her. More than anything, he wanted to trail his lips along the warm silken skin of her throat, to savour that frantically beating pulse, to slide his hands beneath that T-shirt and skim his fingers over the peaks of her breasts. No boundaries. No restraint. No inhibitions.

He took a breath. 'I wish we could stay on the *Alighieri* for ever,' he whispered. 'Just you and me, sailing into a new dawn each day and drifting into the sunset at night.'

But... He didn't say it. He didn't need to.

'But we need to get back,' she said softly.

Watching his face still, Juliet felt her stomach flip over, and just for a few heart-stopping half-seconds she let her hands splay against his back as she felt the rigid press of his erection against her belly.

Heat was radiating through her body—the familiar, electrifying rush of desire for skin on skin, for his taste, his touch...

Only it was so much more than that.

On waking, she had felt memories of what had happened in the early hours of the morning fill her head. Their lovemaking, his panic attack, their conversation... and of course their reconciliation.

The last few days had changed so many things. She had talked to Ralph about her past—really talked—and his unconditional support had helped her to see herself and him in a different light.

But it had been seeing him so desperate, so distressed, or rather the fact that he had let her see him like that, that had blown away all thoughts of divorcing him.

He was her love, her life, her future—with or without a baby in her womb.

In a little over forty-eight hours they would be hosting the biggest party in town *together*—and this time it wouldn't just be an appearance of unity. This time it would be real.

Brushing his lips with her own, she tipped her head back and met his gaze head-on. 'We need to get back for the ball.'

She felt him tense.

The opera festival was a huge deal in Verona, but the Castellucci Ball was legendary in its own right. Not only was it a charitable fundraiser that raised seven-figure sums, it also gave guests a chance to mingle with celebrities from the world of art, fashion, film and music. It was the most important date in the family's social calendar. But she knew that wasn't the reason why his back suddenly felt like a rigid wall of muscle.

'Is Niccolò Farnese going to be there?' she asked quietly.

She knew he would be even before Ralph nodded. The Farneses were a powerful family—not as old as the Castelluccis, but still with connections stretching across Italy and beyond.

'With his wife.' He rubbed a hand across his eyes as if he wanted to block out the facts. 'And obviously Carlo will be there too.' His mouth twisted. 'It feels dangerous…all of us being there together. Like tempting fate.'

Hearing the strain in his voice, she felt a rush of self-loathing that she had considered letting him face this ordeal alone. 'Nothing is going to happen,' she said fiercely. 'I won't let it.'

His arms tightened around her. 'It feels like a betrayal…being there with both of them, neither of them knowing the truth…'

'You're not betraying anyone.' Her heart felt as if it was going to burst. She loved him so much that his pain was her pain. 'This is an impossible situation—nobody would know how to handle it, and most people wouldn't try. They'd just run away and hide.' She could feel his heart beating in time with hers. 'You're not doing that.'

He shifted against her, moving back slightly so that he could see her face.

Tilting her head back, she met his gaze. 'You're putting your feelings aside for Carlo and your family. You're going to smile and greet your guests and give them an evening to remember. And I'll be right by your side.'

He nodded slowly, his fingers curving over her belly. 'I'd like that.'

Her arm brushed against his. 'It's going to be fine. I promise. And when you're ready…when you've figured out how to say what you want to say…you can have a conversation with your father. Both of your fathers,' she said softly.

There was a silence. In the limitless sky above them the sun looked like a child's drawing. She heard him breathe out shakily.

'Thank you for doing this.'

She frowned. 'Doing what?'

He hesitated. 'Putting your feelings aside. I know

you don't really enjoy the whole social scene, and that's partly my fault. No, it *is*,' he said as she started to protest. 'It was a lot to take on for anyone—much less someone who didn't even speak Italian.'

Reaching out, he pushed her hair behind her ear.

'Only I didn't think about that. I was so caught up with not being a Castellucci and I projected that onto you. I'm sorry.'

'I know you are.'

It was enough to know that he cared. She squeezed his hand, and saw his face relax a little.

'So, are you ready to turn the boat around?' she asked.

A shiver ran along his jaw as he glanced past her at the horizon, but then slowly he nodded.

She leaned into him, her heart beating in time with his.

The ramifications of his mother's affair had not been forgotten, but they would deal with it together. One day at a time.

The past was not going to come between them ever again.

CHAPTER NINE

TURNING ON THE SPOT, Juliet gazed into the mirror, her eyes moving critically over her reflection. She turned to the petite dark-haired woman beside her. 'What do you think?'

They were standing in the ornate master bedroom at the *palazzo*, but for once the gilt and marble setting was taking a back seat. Instead, it was the rail of jewel-bright dresses that held centre stage, their intricate beading and lustrous fabrics catching the morning sunlight and spraying rainbows across the room.

'I think you look exquisite. But it's what you think that matters, *cara*.'

Juliet grimaced. 'But I don't know what I think, Gia. That's why I have you.'

Before becoming a personal stylist, Gia Marazzi had worked for two of the largest fashion houses in Italy. Preternaturally calm and exceptionally pretty, Gia was the chicest woman she had ever met. She was also one of the nicest, and had become a friend as well as an advisor.

Gia shook her head. 'You have me because you don't like shopping.'

The look of disbelief on the stylist's perfectly made-up face as she spoke made Juliet burst out laughing. 'So would you if you had to go everywhere with a quartet of heavily armed over-muscular men tracking your every footstep.'

But that wasn't the only reason.

Before she'd met Ralph she'd never had enough money to really enjoy spending it on clothes. Marrying into the Castelluccis had obviously changed that, but even after she'd married Ralph she'd still felt completely out of her depth and horribly conspicuous, so that even thinking about walking into the designer boutiques on Milan's Via Montenapoleone had been a toe-curlingly daunting prospect.

Back then she'd been so unsure of himself.

Or maybe sure only of one thing.

That it was simply a matter of time before Ralph realised the mistake he had made in marrying her. That sooner or later he would see her for who she was, and her fashion choices would just speed up the inevitable exposure.

Her heart bumped gently against her ribs.

Except he had seen who she was.

Sitting with her on that tiny little patch of sand, he had peeled back the layers she wore to protect herself against the world.

He knew who she was now.

He knew her and he wanted her.

The good, the bad, and even the ugly.

Ignoring the fluttering rush of unease that accompanied that resolute thought, she twisted round to face the mirror, holding out the full, heavy skirt.

This dress was the opposite of ugly.

In fact, it seemed ridiculous to criticise something so unspeakably lovely.

But… 'It just feels a little too structured, too emphatic.' She screwed up her face apologetically. 'Sorry, Gia. I know it's your favourite.'

'I do love it.' The stylist laughed. 'But *I'm* not going to be wearing it.' Running her hand lightly over the exquisite lace, Gia narrowed her eyes. 'And I do know what you mean. It's a dress that makes an unequivocal statement.'

'Yes, it does.'

The deep voice made Juliet stop mid-twirl. Glancing over her bare shoulder, she felt her mouth dry. Ralph was leaning against the door frame, his golden gaze fixed on her face, a smile tugging at the corners of his mouth.

Heat scuttled over her skin. Any ordinary man wearing black jeans and a charcoal-grey polo shirt would have looked underdressed beside all the glittering, embellished couture gowns. But that was the difference between Ralph and every other human. He didn't need a stylist or a rack of jaw-droppingly expensive clothes to make heads turn.

'It says my wife is unequivocally the most beautiful woman in the world.'

Juliet watched him walk towards her. 'You like it?'

she asked. Her breath hitched in her throat as Ralph touched her lightly on the hip and she turned to face him.

They had arrived back in Verona yesterday afternoon. It had been a strange sensation, walking back into the *palazzo*—a kind of *déjà-vu*. Her home had seemed so familiar, and yet it had felt inexplicably different. Everything had felt lighter, brighter—almost as if it had been aired and redecorated in the time they'd been away.

But of course nothing had changed in a physical sense. It was just that so much had happened…so many things had changed between her and Ralph.

She felt a shimmer of pure happiness, warm like sunlight on her skin. It was as if the misery and uncertainty of the last few months had been erased and they had gone back to the beginning. Only the difference was that this time they were not stumbling around blindfolded. The past was an open book now.

It had been painful to admit their frailties and their fears, but they had come through the fire together and now they were stronger, wiser.

Closer.

She leaned into him, panic clutching at her stomach as she remembered how close she had come to walking away, to leaving this man who was her life blood, her breath, her heart, her soul.

'I like it a lot,' he said.

His fingers splayed against her waist. They were warm and firm and she felt her panic fade.

'It's a beautiful dress.' He stared down at her appraisingly. 'But I think the fabric is too rigid and the blue is too dark. You need something with a little more fluidity...*and heat*.'

Their eyes met and she sucked in a sharp breath as he brushed past her. Heart pounding, she watched as he pulled out a soft, swirling mass of primrose-coloured silk from the rail.

'That was my first choice,' she said softly. 'And I do really like it. But we thought it was a bit too sunny...'

'And you want moonlight?' he said softly, his eyes locking with hers. 'And music, and love, and romance? Isn't that how the song goes?'

Her stomach flipped over. When he looked at her like that there was no need to go to the opera. She could almost hear an orchestra playing.

'So...' his hand rested on a long silk jersey dress the colour of ripe Morello cherries '...how about this one?'

'Now, that was my first choice,' Gia purred approvingly.

Five minutes later Juliet was staring at her reflection again, and this time she didn't need to ask anyone how she looked. She could see the heat glittering in Ralph's eyes, and feel an answering heat flickering low in her belly as his gaze drifted over the smooth red silk.

'Yes,' he said quietly as she turned slowly on the spot.

The air hissed between them.

Yes, she thought silently.

From the front the dress looked simple enough—modest, even, with its long sleeves and boat neckline. But from behind the fluid fabric was cut to a tantalising bottom-skimming V.

It was Gia who broke the pulsing silence. 'I think

we can all agree that in this instance less is definitely more,' she said, with undisguised satisfaction.

Picking up her handbag, she sashayed across the room, kissed Juliet, and lifted her face for Ralph to graze her cheek.

'Clearly my services are no longer required, so I'll see you both at the Arena.' She paused. 'Unless you need help with your accessories?'

Shaking her head, Juliet took hold of Ralph's hand, a small smile tugging at the corners of her mouth. 'Thanks, Gia, but I already have the best accessory.'

There was a slight click as the door closed behind her. Ralph took a step forward and caught her against him, his hand low and flat on her back. Slowly she looked up into his face.

'Hi,' he said softly.

'Hi,' she whispered.

And then his mouth found hers and she felt her body turn boneless as he kissed her softly.

When they broke apart she caught his arms, her fingers pressing against the heat of his skin. 'I missed you.'

His lips curved up at the corners. 'I missed you too.'

Pulling her close, he rubbed his face against hers. The heat of his body and the warm, clean scent of his skin was making her head spin.

'I don't know how I'm ever going to go back to work,' he murmured. 'I can't bear being apart from you.'

The steady burn of his gaze made her an ache grow in her stomach. 'I can't bear it either.'

She could say that now—could admit her need for him without fearing that it was all they shared.

Which was lucky. Because right now it was a need that was making her feel as if she was melting from the inside out.

'I'd better get this dress back on the hanger.' Lifting the skirt with her foot, she flicked it to one side and cleared her throat. 'Could you help me?'

There was a slight pause, and then he nodded. 'With pleasure,' he said softly, moving closer.

His hands were gentle but firm as he turned her away from him, and her skin twitched as his fingers slid over the smooth fabric to the concealed zip.

As he pulled the dress down over her shoulders she felt her pulse accelerate. 'Wait a minute.' Grabbing the frame of the bed for balance, she bent over. 'Let me take my shoes off—'

He caught her wrist. 'No, keep them on.'

Ralph held his breath as she looked up at him, her soft brown eyes wide with longing, her cheeks flushed with the same hunger that was turning his body to stone.

He'd been on the phone all morning, going over the last-minute arrangements for the ball tomorrow. When he'd gone looking for Giulietta he'd actually forgotten that she would be trying on dresses with Gia. He'd just wanted to see her…to hear her voice. To touch base.

Only now he was with her he wanted to do so much more.

He wanted to kiss and caress and lick and stroke and tease.

Reaching out, he slid the dress slowly down over her stomach, holding her steady as she stepped free of the silky fabric. Now she was naked except for her simple white panties, and his eyes abseiled jerkily down her thighs to her skin-toned patent high heels.

For a moment he forgot to breathe. His body ached— *hell*, even his teeth ached because he wanted her so badly.

Her breasts were quivering slightly, the nipples already taut beneath his gaze, and as the blood surged down to his groin he thought he might actually pass out.

Almost without conscious thought, he slid one hand to the nape of her neck. The other moved to cup her breast as he kissed her softly, then more fiercely as he felt the slide of her tongue against his own.

His fingers moved from her breast to her hip and then, pushing past the waistband of her panties, he parted her thighs and with the delicate, measured precision of a *maestro pasticcere* found the nub of her clitoris.

He bit back a groan as her hand found his and she pressed his fingers against the damp fabric. She was already so wet for him.

Dropping to his knees, he slid his hands beneath her panties and pulled them gently down her legs. He took a breath, inhaling her scent. Then, resting his head against the cotton-soft skin of her thigh, his hands gripping her bottom to hold her steady, he traced a path between the dark curls, his flattened tongue merciless as she opened herself to him.

Her hands caught in his hair and he heard the sudden hitch in her breath, and then she was pulling him closer, crying out as she spasmed against his mouth. 'Let me!'

His erection was straining against the front of his jeans and she unzipped him, and then she was pushing him urgently onto the bed, her fingers wrapping around his fully aroused length.

'Ah, Giulietta…'

He breathed out her name, his fingers moving automatically to grip her hair as she knelt down in front of him and he felt her mouth slide over the swollen, heavy head of his erection.

Looking down, he felt his breath hiss between his teeth as he watched her guide him in, inch by inch.

When she ran her tongue over the raised ridge of his frenulum, he grunted. His head was swimming and his body felt as if it was dissolving, unravelling, the tug of her mouth acting with the gravitational force of a black hole.

He pulled out, panting, his heart raging, and then, standing up unsteadily, he turned her so that she was bending over the bed. Gazing down at the curve of her back, he felt his body tighten unbearably. He gripped her hips—and then he remembered.

'Don't move,' he said hoarsely. 'I'm just going to grab—'

'No.' She caught his hand. 'No. I don't—we don't need to. I don't want to.'

Her eyes were soft and dazed.

'Are you sure?'

She gave him an open-mouthed kiss by way of assent, and he kissed her back fiercely, drawing her up against his body.

Shivers of anticipation were rippling over her skin

and, heart hammering, he pressed his erection against the soft cushion of her bottom. He lifted her hips and she backed up to meet him. Reaching under her stomach, he found her breast, brushing a thumb over the nipple, feeling it swell and harden.

Her soft moan acted like gasoline on the flames of his desire and, shifting slightly, he eased into her in one smooth movement. As her slick heat enveloped him he felt his control snap. His hands splayed against her back and he began to thrust inside her.

Moaning, she rocked against him, meeting his thrusts, her breath staccato, her whole body shaking now. He thrust harder and she gasped. He felt her jerk against him, and then he felt her fingers cupping him, squeezing gently, and he was jerking against her, a jagged cry jamming his throat, his body spilling into hers with molten force.

Breathing raggedly, he eased out of her and they both collapsed on the bed together.

He understood the significance of what they had just done—what she had allowed him to do.

It was a sign—a physical demonstration of her commitment to him, to their future, and the fact that she felt that way made an ache swell behind his ribs. The fact that she trusted him enough to show him so candidly, so passionately, almost undid him.

'What are you thinking about?' she asked,

Her hand was pressed against his shirt and, looking down, he saw that she was searching his face. In the past when she'd asked him that question he'd usually changed the subject. Or kissed her. Sometimes both.

But now he gently smoothed her hair from her face and met her gaze.

'I was thinking about us. About how we met. About why I stopped that day.'

Her mouth tugged up at one corner. 'You're a gentleman and you saw a woman in distress.'

He frowned. 'No, that can't be it. I wasn't actually sure you were human, let alone female.'

'Hey!' She punched him lightly on the arm and he started laughing.

'To be fair, you looked like a drowned cat.' He caught her arm and pulled her closer. 'But you're right—I did think you needed help.'

His heart turned over as he remembered the electrifying jolt that had gone through his body, the absolute, unshakeable certainty that she was *the one*.

Reaching down, he brushed her cheek with his thumb. 'Only I was wrong. You were rescuing me.'

His life had been in a tailspin. But this woman—this beautiful, strong, loyal woman—had faced her own fears to stop him crash landing.

She stared at him steadily. 'We rescued each other.'

He brushed his lips across hers. 'And one very savage and ungrateful cat,' he said softly, gathering her against him as she buried her face in his shoulder, shaking with laughter.

For Juliet, the past twenty-four hours had seemed to pass in the space of a heartbeat, and now they were fast approaching the hour when the beautiful mirror-lined ballroom would be filled with guests.

But right now the room was empty.

The team in charge of staging the ball had worked almost non-stop to get everything in place, and from the polished parquet floor to the frescoed ceiling it all looked quite magical.

After the frantic efforts of the last few days, the silence now was intense, almost vertiginous. Or maybe that was guilt, she thought, glancing at the Rococo clock that stood at the end of the room.

Everyone else was busy getting ready. Glancing down at her cashmere robe and slippered feet, she bit her lip. She should be getting ready too. But she had wanted a private sneaky peek.

Turning slowly on the spot, she felt a rush of satisfaction.

Burnished silver bowls were filled with the palest pink roses, chandeliers glittered and the huge velvet curtains were beautifully swagged. All of it looked perfect.

Somewhere in the house a door slammed, and her heart started beating a little faster.

This year it needed to be more perfect than ever.

This year would be the first time in thirty years that the ball for three hundred carefully selected guests would not be hosted by Francesca and Carlo Castellucci.

This year she and Ralph would have that honour.

She felt a lurch of panic, as if the marble floor she was standing on had turned to ice.

Panic was understandable, she told herself quickly. It was not just an honour, but a responsibility.

Her breath caught in her throat. She should be feeling happy, and she had been happy back on the *Alighi-*

eri, a kind of sweet, piercing happiness that had felt unassailable.

Her hand curved against her stomach. Whatever the future held, they would face it together.

Together.

Except the word seemed slippery, treacherous, unsteady—as if she was holding something that was too big for her hands, so that it was always on the verge of sliding between her fingers.

She glanced nervously up at the paintings above the mirrors, feeling the cool, assessing gaze of Ralph's ancestors.

It had been building, this feeling, as the hour of the ball had got ever closer. The familiar shifting doubts had been closing in on her like early-evening shadows. And now they were rising up and threatening to swallow her whole.

Turning away from the paintings, she glanced down at the name cards on the nearest table, her heart pounding as she read the beautiful italic writing.

Il Signor Castellucci
La Signora Castellucci

She took a deep breath, striving for calm.

It was crazy to feel so insecure, so inadequate.

She was married to the most glamorous man in the world—a man she loved, a man who loved her. And they had a seamless, innate understanding of each other, like skaters moving together with smooth synchronicity across a frozen lake.

Her chest ached sharply, as if she'd run out of breath.

Of course it was easy to spin and turn and leap when it was just the two of you on the ice. It would be harder when there were other people around to get in your way and trip you up.

But Ralph would be there to catch her if she fell. He had told her that—just as he had told her that he wanted *every* possible version of her. There was nothing to fear. Not from their guests and certainly not from a bunch of oil paintings.

From somewhere inside the house she heard the sound of voices coming from where Roberto was briefing the assembled waiting staff.

Her stomach fluttered. What was she doing? Standing here half-dressed with her hair in rollers, unpicking herself?

Tonight was a celebration. Plus, Anna was probably already upstairs, waiting to do her hair and make-up.

Blanking her mind, she turned and made her way back through the *palazzo*.

Forty minutes later the rollers were gone and in their place was a sleek, sculptured chignon.

All she had to do now was put on her dress.

Heart hammering, she checked her appearance in the mirror in their bedroom.

'It's got the night off.'

A ripple of quicksilver ran down her spine and she turned to where Ralph stood, watching her. Heat pulsed across her skin.

The first time she'd seen him in an evening suit she'd felt as though the world had tilted on its axis. And nothing had changed, she thought, her fingers gripping the chest of drawers to steady herself.

He wore a dark classic single-button tuxedo with peaked lapels, a white French-cuffed dress shirt, and superbly tailored trousers that hung perfectly to graze the tops of his handmade black Oxfords.

She frowned. 'I don't understand…'

He walked slowly towards her, his face unsmiling. 'The mirror. Not that you need to ask.' Reaching out, he touched her cheek gently. 'You are the fairest in the land.' His eyes held hers and then he smiled. 'But I think there's something missing.'

Reaching into his pocket, he pulled out a small square box. Her pulse stumbled as he flipped it open to reveal a pair of dark red pear-cut ruby earrings.

'Ralph, you didn't have to,' she whispered, touching them lightly. 'Oh, but they're so beautiful.'

He stared at her steadily. 'No, *you're* beautiful. They're just baubles.'

As she put the earrings on her eyes met his in the reflection of the mirror, and the slow, lambent burn of his gaze made her skin feel hot and tight.

Reaching out, he flicked one of the delicate jewels with his finger, and she felt her pulse beat in time with the oscillating pendant.

'You're going to be the belle of the ball tonight. But you're always my *bella* Giulietta.'

She felt her stomach clench. More than anything she wanted to believe him. To believe that she had a right to be here, to be his wife. *Unconditionally.*

Smiling back at his reflection, she cleared her throat. 'You scrub up pretty well yourself.'

His answering smile seemed to press down on her pubic bone and suddenly, illogically, breathing made her breathless.

'Thank you for these, Ralph.'

He was standing behind her, so close she could feel his warm breath feathering the nape of her neck. The weight of his hand felt sensual, intimate, possessive...

'It's my pleasure,' he said softly.

She felt his fingers splay against the bare skin of her back and lightning skittered down her spine. It would be so easy to move her head a little, to turn into him and seek his lips, to lose herself and her fears in the firm, insistent press of his mouth...

He groaned. 'Don't look at me like that, *bella*.'

She bit her lip. 'Sorry.'

'No, I'm sorry.' A muscle tightened in his jaw. 'I'm just a bit tense.'

'It's going to be fine.' The desperation she'd heard in his voice, his willingness to share his fear, made her fingers tighten around his. 'I'll be there to make sure it is.'

It hurt her—hurt with a debilitating relentless intensity—to know that she had come so close to breaking that vow that she had let her fears and insecurities come between them.

'I wish—' He screwed up his face, stopped.

'Wish what?' She looked up at him, and kept looking until he shook his head.

'It's stupid. I just wish we knew about the baby already.'

She felt his words, and the longing in his eyes, tug at her heart. She felt the same way. The thought of walking into the Verona Arena knowing that she was carrying Ralph's child almost undid her. She wanted it so badly.

They both did.

As he pulled her against him his phone buzzed from across the room. It would be Marco, letting them know that the car was ready for them.

'I'll tell him we need a bit longer,' she said quickly. Her head was buzzing. Her throat felt as though it was closing up.

'No, it's fine.' Catching her hand in his, he lifted it to his mouth and kissed it gently. 'I'm ready if you are.'

For one wild moment she wanted to ask him whether this was real. Whether all this intimacy and certainty would fade like it had before, after Rome.

But she was being stupid.

Ralph had made it clear that he loved her—every version of her.

He'd told her that.

And, yes, they were just words, but they had come from the heart and she needed to trust in them. To trust in him and their incredible intuitive understanding of each other.

Stomach lurching, she steadied her nerves and forced a smile. 'I am.'

The journey into the city was surprisingly swift. As VIPs, the Castelluccis had a police escort, and they were waved past the lines of traffic.

The opera was packed—a sell-out, in fact. Fourteen

thousand people waiting excitedly for a performance of *La Traviata*.

She had never seen so many people—so many beautiful, well-connected people—but she didn't care. There was only one face that mattered to her.

But she could sense that her husband was searching the crowd for one face.

Her pulse accelerated. She knew that, for him, tonight was not just about 'moonlight and music and love and romance'. It was about putting ghosts to rest and making a silent, heartfelt prayer for the future.

She felt Ralph's hand tense in hers as Carlo Castellucci stepped towards them, handsome in his dark suit.

'*Ciao*, Giulietta, *mia cara*, you look divine. Ralph, *mio figlio*.'

Watching the two men embrace, she felt her tears sting her eyes. Whatever their DNA might say, they were father and son, and she knew that nothing, not even the truth, could come between them.

But would that be true for her and Ralph?

Suddenly she was struggling not to cry, and it was a relief when the orchestra began to tune up and they took their seats.

Darkness fell, and the hum of voices settled into silence It was time to light the *mocoleto*—the candles handed out to the audience in homage to the ancient history of the Arena as a place of entertainment.

'Here.' Ralph bent forward, lighting her candle with his.

'Ralph, I just need to—'

'I know I don't—'

They both spoke at once.

She stared at him, her heart beating fast and out of time. 'You first,' she said quickly.

Their eyes met above the tiny, fluttering flames.

'I know I don't say it enough,' he said, 'but I love you, Giulietta. You…our baby…' he rested his hand against her stomach '…you're everything I've ever wanted.'

In the flickering circle of light, his face was so serious, so beautiful, so essential to her. She could hear the hope, the yearning in his voice, and then she thought about the excruciating loneliness she'd felt in London.

Her mouth was dry, her throat tight.

She couldn't ask him now if he'd meant what he said—couldn't break the spell of his words.

Instead she leaned into him, their mouths fusing as the beautiful, sweeping score by Verdi rose from the orchestra pit and soared upwards to the starry sky.

CHAPTER TEN

GAZING AROUND THE crowded ballroom, Ralph knew he should be feeling satisfied with how the evening was progressing—and part of him was more than satisfied.

Everything was going exactly as planned.

The tables from dinner had been cleared away and waiters with trays of drinks were moving smoothly between the women in their shimmering dresses and the men in their monochromatic evening wear. Beneath the ornate Venetian glass chandeliers people were dancing and talking and laughing.

All that remained was for him to introduce the auction. But tonight was always going to be about more than giving people a good time and raising money.

This was Francesca Castellucci's event.

His mother had started it in the first year of her marriage and, thanks to her, it had grown from being a small soirée for family and friends to a major social event.

Glancing across the room, he felt his shoulders tense.

His mother had not only been beautiful and vivacious, she'd made things happen—only for months now he'd been struggling to come to terms with some of those things.

But stepping into her shoes this evening had made him understand her more, had made him realise that she hadn't been just his mother. She had been a woman with strengths and flaws.

And he missed her. Every day.

Only thanks to the woman walking towards him now he'd been able to face the past and move forward in his life to embrace the wonderful present.

He glanced over at Giulietta, his eyes lingering on her flat stomach beneath the clinging silk of her dress. Being here with her tonight was not just about the present, but the future—a new and exciting future. A future that might already be growing inside her.

His heart began to beat a little faster.

He'd wanted a baby before, but back then it had only been a possibility. Here, tonight, at the ball founded by his mother and with both his fathers in attendance, it felt more real, somehow, and more insistent. It was a wordless, elemental need to have something of his own—a continuation of his bloodline.

'Are you okay?' Her hand found his.

He was having to lean into her to make himself heard above the hum of laughter and conversation, and as her warm breath grazed her throat he felt a flicker of corresponding heat in his groin.

He had a strong urge to scoop her into his arms and carry her upstairs. To lose himself in the heat and intensity of their coupling.

But he was a little bit older and wiser now.

Refusing to face the past had nearly destroyed his marriage and he would not make the same mistake again. And his past was here in this room.

Both the *passato prossimo* and the *imperfecto*.

His gaze travelled from Carlo Castellucci to where Niccolò Farnese stood, with his wife Marina and his daughter Vittoria—Ralph's half-sister—his head bent in conversation with the lead tenor from the evening's performance.

As though sensing his gaze, Vittoria looked up and smiled across the room, but then his heart bumped against his ribs as he realised that his half-sister wasn't smiling at him, but at Juliet. And his wife was smiling too.

Reaching out, he caught her by the waist, his thumbs gently brushing over the smooth silk of her dress. 'I'm better than okay,' he said softly.

There was a clinking of silver on glass, and a hush fell on the room. Turning, Ralph saw that Carlo was standing slightly apart, a glass and a knife in his hand.

'I know this year I've taken a bit of a back seat in the arrangements for our family's annual ball, but I hope Ralph won't mind if I say a few words before the start of tonight's auction.'

It wasn't on the running order, but Ralph shook his head. 'Of course not, Papà.'

Carlo smiled. 'Thank you—and thank you to all of you for coming here tonight. As you know, the money raised goes to the charitable foundation set up by my late wife, and it really does make a difference to people's lives.'

He waited for the enthusiastic applause to die down and then began speaking again.

'I miss Francesca,' he said simply. 'And I don't think I will ever not miss her. But it's not Francesca I want to talk about tonight. It's my son, Ralph, without whose strength and support I would have gone under.'

Ralph felt a tug at his heart as Carlo turned to face him.

'I'm in no need of charity, but he makes a difference to my life every day, and I don't think I've made that clear enough. So I'd like to remedy that now, if I may.' Holding up his glass, his father smiled across the room. 'To Ralph. For making a difference to me.'

As everyone lifted their glasses and repeated the toast Ralph felt a sharp sting of love and guilt for the man who had raised him.

Voices were buzzing in his head. Suddenly it was an effort to breathe. He felt dizzy—nauseous, almost.

He hid it well. His handsome face was smooth, and a smile pulled at his mouth so that nobody would know he was deeply moved.

Except Giulietta.

Without thinking, he leaned into her soft body and kissed her.

'It's okay,' she whispered softly against his mouth. 'It's okay.'

He pulled her closer, his fingers seeking the curve of her spine like a rock climber searching for a hand-hold. The pain in his chest felt as if it would never leave.

'Ralph…'

It was Carlo, smiling, calm.

'Sorry, Giulietta. I wonder if it would be possible to have a quick word with my son? I promise not to keep him long.'

Beside him, he felt Giulietta nod.

'Of course. There's someone I've been meaning to speak to all evening,' she said quickly, squeezing his hand before she let it go. 'Take as long as you need.'

As long as you need.

The words echoed inside his head as he followed Carlo into the drawing room, where he'd imagined them talking so many times in his dreams. But how long would it take before he would be ready to honour this man with the truth?

He shut the door, expecting his father to sit down, but instead Carlo walked over to where someone—probably Roberto—had put out a decanter of whisky and two glasses.

Clearly his father had planned this… His heart began to pound. Except Carlo didn't drink whisky as a rule.

'Here.' His father held out a glass. 'I hope you don't mind me taking you away from the party—it's just that we haven't seen much of one another lately, and…well, tonight is your mother's night. It always will be.'

Ralph nodded, his chest tightening at the hollowed-out note in his father's usually polished voice. 'I know, Papà.'

Carlo smiled unsteadily. 'I let her down, Ralph.'

'No!' The word exploded from his lips as he shook his head. 'You loved her, Papà. You took care of her.'

'Yes, I did.' His father nodded, his smile fading. 'But I still let her down. You see, she asked me to do something…something important…and I haven't. I couldn't. I was too scared. Too scared of losing you too.'

Ralph frowned. His head felt strange, flimsy and thin, as if it were made of paper. 'I don't understand, Papà.'

Except he did.

Around him the room seemed to fold in on itself, and he gripped the back of an armchair to get his balance back.

'You know,' he said shakily.

'That I'm not your biological father? Yes.'

There was a brightness to Carlo's eyes as he nodded. 'Your mother told me just after she found out she was pregnant with you.' His mouth twisted. 'I know you're angry with her, and that's completely understandable. But please don't judge her. She made a bad choice and she was so ashamed. That's why she found it so hard to talk to you about it.' Carlo's gaze was clear and unflinching. 'But we were both at fault, Ralph.'

Ralph met his father's eyes. 'I believe you.'

Marriages might look balanced to an outsider, but he knew from his own experience that they were a perpetually shifting equation of power and need and expectation.

'But we never stopped loving one another, and both of us wanted to make our marriage—*our family*—work.' Carlo took a deep breath. 'That's why we decided not to tell you until you were old enough to understand. And, of course, Niccolò and Marina had started their own family.'

'Vittoria…' Ralph said quietly.

'Yes, Vittoria.' Carlo gave him a small, stiff smile. 'When she came to the house your mother was devastated. She had no idea that Niccolò had kept those letters.' Reaching out, Carlo gripped Ralph's arm. 'She hated it that you found out that way. It was wrong, and unfair, and we should have told you. I know that now, and there's no excuse except that we both loved you so much and were scared of how you'd react.'

Ralph saw that tears were sliding down his father's handsome face.

'Before she died she made me promise to tell you everything—only I couldn't make myself do it.'

'I should have come to you.' Ralph didn't even try to hide the emotion in his voice. 'I should have talked to you.'

'*No.*' Carlo was shaking his head. 'You've grown into a fine young man but I'm the adult here, and you'll always be my child...*my son.*' He took another breath. 'That is if you still want to be.'

Ralph couldn't speak, but words were unnecessary for what he needed to say and, stepping forward, he embraced his father.

Carlo's arms hugged him close. 'I want you to know that I will support you in everything you want to do—including getting to know Niccolò.' Loosening his grip, he smiled shakily. 'And your mother felt the same way.'

'Thank you, Papà.'

'No, thank *you*, *mio figlio.*' His father squeezed his shoulder. 'And believe me when I say that you *are* a Castellucci, Ralph. Our family bond goes beyond blood and that in the end is all that matters: family.'

Ralph felt his heart swell. More than anything, he wanted to tell his father that Giulietta might be pregnant. It would be the perfect gift to repay Carlo's love and loyalty. A chance to demonstrate his own love and commitment to the family that had raised him.

But he would need to run it past Juliet first…

After Carlo and Ralph had left the ballroom, Juliet turned and walked over to where a dark-haired woman with eyes like her husband was looking up at a beautiful Titian.

'Vittoria,' she said quietly.

'Juliet.'

There had been no need for introductions as both women had reached out to embrace each other.

As they stepped apart, Vittoria held on to Juliet's hand. 'I'm so sorry for the trouble I've caused. When I found the letters I freaked out. I thought Ralph was the only one who would understand, and he was so kind and patient.'

She screwed up her face.

'Only I didn't think about how it would look. I didn't think about anything or anyone but myself.'

Her fingers tightened around Juliet's.

'Do you think you can forgive me?'

'Of course I can forgive you,' Juliet said gently.

How could she not?

Up close, the similarities between the half-siblings were subtle, but irrefutable—the shape and colour of their eyes, the line of their noses…

'You were thinking about your family. And, actually, you did me—both of us—a favour.'

Breathing out shakily, Vittoria glanced over her shoulder. 'I should be getting back. My father wants me to bid on that BVLGARI bracelet. It's a surprise for my mum so he's taken her out to see the gardens.' She smiled. 'But perhaps we could go out to lunch one day.'

Juliet took a quick breath, steadied her voice. 'I'd like that. I'd like that very much.'

She watched Vittoria leave, then turned back to look up at the Titian. She had been terrified to approach Vittoria, but now she was glad she'd done it. Perhaps they might even become friends.

'There you are…'

Ralph was by her side. 'Ralph, I was—' she began, but he caught her hand.

'I need to talk to you.'

She searched his face, his eyes, and knew without having to ask that he had told his father the truth.

Heart hammering, she let him lead her through the house and up the stairs to their bedroom. As he pushed the door shut he turned and clasped her face, his thumbs stroking her cheeks as he stared down at her.

Her hands gripped his arms. His whole body was trembling. 'You told him, didn't you?' she said gently. 'About not being his son.'

She felt his shoulders shift, the muscles in his chest tighten.

'I didn't have to. He already knew.'

'I don't understand…' She stared at him, blinking.

'My mother told him right at the start when she found

out she was pregnant. She told him she'd had an affair, and that she wanted to try and make things work between them.'

She bit into her lip. 'And they did.' Tears filled her eyes. 'They must have loved each other very much.'

'They did.' His mouth twisted. 'You know that was the hardest thing for me—thinking that it had all been a sham, an act. But it wasn't.'

She gripped his arms more tightly. 'I'm so happy for you, Ralph—and for Carlo.'

He breathed out shakily. 'They did think about telling me the truth, but then Niccolò and Marina had Vittoria, and everyone seemed happy.'

She nodded. 'I talked to Vittoria. She's really nice.'

'She is. She found it hard at the beginning…' He paused, his eyes locking with hers. 'But she's like all the women in my life. Strong and smart.'

She shook her head. 'You did this, Ralph, not me. It was you and Carlo.'

'No, I couldn't have done it without you. I would have just kept on burying myself in work and pushing you away.' His arm tightened around her waist. 'You pushed back. You made me realise that if I didn't deal with my past I'd lose everything.' He touched her stomach lightly. 'And I have so much to lose.'

His eyes on hers were bright with unshed tears of love and longing.

'Not just our marriage, but our future.' He breathed out shakily. 'It was so hard not telling him that you could be pregnant. I didn't say anything, but I know it would mean so much to him. I thought perhaps we could call him from the clinic.'

The eagerness in his voice made her shake inside. But, forcing a smile to her face, she nodded, and he slid his hand round the nape of her neck, drawing her close.

For a moment they just leaned into one another, his tears mingling with hers. She couldn't breathe. Her throat seemed to have shrunk, so that it felt as if she was having to squeeze her words out.

'So, how does Carlo feel about you talking to Niccolò?'

'He understands why I'd want to, and I will talk to him...'

'But not tonight?'

Their eyes met and he shook his head, his mouth tipping up at one corner. 'No, not tonight. I have other priorities—' He broke off, his face tensing as he glanced down at his watch. 'Like the auction.'

'So go.' She pressed her hands against his chest. 'Go on. I'm just going to tidy myself up a bit and then I'll follow.'

'Are you sure?' He looked uncertain.

'Of course. I'll be down in a minute. Go.'

Left alone, she walked into the bathroom and held her hands under the cold tap. Thanks to Anna, her mascara hadn't run, but she could feel her pulse leaping in her wrists.

Lifting her head, she stared at her face. Like most girls growing up, she had pored over pictures of her favourite celebrities, thinking that if only she could look like them her life would be different...*better*.

Now, though, staring at her own glossy lips, her smoky eyes and artfully flushed cheeks, she knew that anyone could look the part. It was how you felt on the inside that mattered.

And she felt as if everything was crumbling to dust... all her hopes and certainties.

She turned off the tap, watching the water spiral down the plughole. For so long she had been scared of the past. Scared of repeating her parents' mistakes, of becoming a person she didn't want to be against her will.

Now, though, she could see that the past wasn't the threat. It was the present. The here and now. The person she was.

And if that person wasn't carrying Ralph's baby, what then?

Her heart pounded like a cannon against her ribs.

Earlier in the ballroom, before the ball had started, she'd reminded herself that Ralph had told her he loved her—every version of her.

And he'd been telling the truth. She knew that. Speaking from the heart.

But what his heart wanted more than anything was for her to be pregnant.

Only what would happen if she wasn't?

They had grown so close in the past few days— surely nothing could come between them.

Except it had after Rome.

And how could she be sure that it wouldn't again?

How could she be sure of anything?

Her whole life had been spent second-guessing her parents, and how many times had she got it wrong?

She couldn't breathe. Everything was tangling inside her.

If only she could talk to someone.

Not Ralph. She couldn't bear even thinking that she might see doubt in his face, distance in his eyes.

There was no one. She was alone.

'*Sold!* To Signor Gino Rosso. *Grazie*, Gino.' Smiling, Ralph banged the gavel down as a ripple of applause filled the ballroom. 'And now, I'm going to hand over to my cousin, Felix. But please keep bidding, people. Remember, it's all for a very good cause.'

Still smiling, Ralph made his way through the tables and chairs, his eyes fixed on the huge double doors at the end of the room. But as he left the ballroom his smile faded. After the noise of the ball the house felt oddly silent, and he glanced down at his watch, frowning.

It had been at least thirty minutes since he'd left Giulietta upstairs, and he'd half expected to meet her on her way to find him. Only the hallway was empty.

His shoulders tensed. Surely it couldn't take her that long to tidy herself up?

There was no reason to think that anything was wrong, but he still took the stairs two at a time.

Their bedroom was in darkness and, switching on the lights, he saw that it was empty. The bathroom was empty too, and for a moment he stood in the doorway, unsure of what to do.

And then a chill slid over his skin as he realised the doors to the balcony were open.

And then he was walking swiftly, fear blotting out all thought.

'Giulietta,' he said hoarsely.

She was sitting on the marble floor, hugging her knees, face lowered.

His limbs felt like lead, but his thoughts were spinning uncontrollably. *Had she hurt herself? Was she ill?*

He was by her side in three strides. Crouching down, he touched her gently. 'What is it, *bella*? Are you okay?'

As she looked up at him a tear rolled down her cheek. He felt her pain inside him, and it was more terrible than anything he'd ever experienced because it was *her* pain.

He sat down beside her and pulled her onto his lap. Holding her close, he let her cry, his fingertips drawing slow circles against her hair until finally a shuddering breath broke from her throat.

'Tell me what it is and I will fix it,' he told her.

She shook her head. 'You can't fix it, Ralph.'

Her voice sounded small and cramped, and a thin sweat spread over his body. 'Then I'll fight it.'

He stared at her, the muscles in his arms bunching. He was desperate to do something—anything—to take away the pain in her voice.

Shaking her head again, she breathed in a shaky breath. 'You can't fight it. It's me.'

His heart jumped. There was something about her posture, the way she was curled in on herself, as though she was trying to hold on to something. Or had already lost it.

'Has something happened?'

She looked up at him, her gaze searching his face. 'You mean with the baby?'

'I suppose I do,' he said quietly. 'But if something's happened to the baby, then it's happened to you too, *bella*.'

Reaching out, Ralph stroked her face gently. Fresh tears spilled down her cheeks.

'Nothing's happened,' she said. 'But what if it had? What if it does?'

She looked down, biting her lip. 'I know how much you want this baby to be real, Ralph. I know how important it is right now for you and your father, for your family...'

He brought her closer against him. 'I do want this baby to be real for my father, and for us, but—'

He swallowed, remembering what it had felt like to walk into their bedroom and find it empty that first time, and then again tonight. Seeing her curled up in a ball like that had been even more devastating.

Burying his face against her hair, he breathed out shakily. 'But when I found you I wasn't thinking about the baby. I thought you were hurt,' he whispered. 'And I didn't care anything else. You're all that matters to me.'

It was true.

Downstairs, with Carlo, the idea of a baby had seemed so urgent to him, so imperative—only now he realised that this woman, their love was enough.

'But what about...?' She hesitated, her eyes seeking

his. 'Will you mind if I'm not pregnant? I mean, I know that's the reason—'

'It was never the reason.' He cupped her face in his hands and kissed her softly. 'You're the reason, *bella*. I love you. Yes, I want you to be pregnant, but if you're not then we'll try again. And if you can't get pregnant then we'll adopt.' His expression gentled. 'In fact, we should do that anyway.'

For a few seconds Ralph rested his forehead against hers, and she felt her heart slow in time with his.

'My life is so blessed already, and I'm sorry that I made you feel that it wasn't—that you weren't enough. Because you are.' His hand moved gently through her hair. 'And I'd give up all of this in a heartbeat, for you.'

She glanced out at the beautiful moonlit grounds. 'You don't need to go that far,' she said, letting a teasing smile tug at the corners of her mouth.

The answering gleam in his eyes seemed to push through her skin.

Reaching out and gripping his jacket, she drew him closer. 'I love you. Ralph. I never stopped loving you, even when I didn't want to—even when I was scared to love you.'

Above them, the sky was starting to grow pale.

His golden gaze drifted slowly across her face, searching, seeing everything. She felt his love warm her skin, filling her with heat, and she closed her eyes against another hot rush of tears.

'E ti amo, Giulietta,' he said softly, drawing her face

close to his. 'You're my sun, my light, my life. Whatever happens, you're all I need. For ever.'

Juliet gazed up at his face…a face that was as familiar, as necessary to her as the sun now rising behind the hills.

And her love for him was as eternal as his for her. Feeling the first rays of light reach over the balcony she leaned into his body, closing her eyes as his mouth found hers.

EPILOGUE

'THERE YOU ARE.' Lucia rushed forward. 'We were getting worried. I thought we might have to send out a search party.'

Shaking his head, Luca shifted Raffaelle from one arm to the other. 'I wasn't worried.'

Smiling, Juliet leaned in to kiss her friend. 'Sorry. Honestly, everything that could go wrong did. We woke up late. I dripped nail polish on my dress. Then Charlie wanted a feed…' She held up her face for Luca to kiss her, and then bent down to kiss Raffaelle. 'Hi, Rafi. And then we had to change him.'

'By "we" she means *me*.'

Turning, Juliet felt a rush of love. Ralph was standing beside her. But it wasn't just her tall, dark, handsome and dangerously tempting husband who was making her heart swell.

It was the beautiful dark-haired baby in his arms.

She felt Ralph's gaze on her face, the tight focus of his clear, golden-eyed love, and with it a vertiginous rush of happiness brighter and more vivid than the stained-glass windows of the church.

It was nearly a year since that week when she and Ralph had found their way back to one another. A week that had started with doubt and despair and ended with hope and reconciliation.

But not with a pregnancy.

Remembering that moment in the clinic when Dr de Masi had told them the test was negative, she drew a breath. She had wept. But Ralph had held her close and told her how much he loved her and needed her, and that when it was meant to happen it would.

And it had.

Two months later she'd been pregnant.

And nine months after that Charles Francesco Castellucci had been born.

And today was his christening.

Not the usual Castellucci christening, with half the world's media tripping over themselves for a photo, but a small, private ceremony for just close friends and the family.

And they were her family too.

Ralph had been determined to make that happen— determined, too, to build on the positives from his own experience for the next generation of Castelluccis.

At that moment, the youngest member of that generation gave a short, imperious shout.

She bent over her son, breathing in his scent. He stared up at her, his small fist pressed against Ralph's shirt, his golden eyes widening as she dropped a kiss on his forehead.

'Are you ready?'

Looking up, she met Ralph's gaze. They had come so

far, she thought. A year ago they had been separated by doubt and mistrust, facing their fears alone. Now they had no secrets. They talked all the time. And they still hadn't run out of ways to say, 'I love you.'

Leaning into him, she caught his arm. 'Yes, we should go in.' She smiled. 'Your fathers will be waiting.'

Ralph put his hand lightly on her hip bone and drew her against his body.

His fathers.

A year ago he had been falling apart. Everything he had taken for granted in his life had been in question. He'd felt torn, conflicted, guilty—and excruciatingly lonely.

Living what had felt like a lie, but terrified of the truth, he'd avoided his family and pushed Giulietta to the point of leaving him.

But she had made him fight for what he wanted.

And she had fought with him. For him. For them.

Without her he would still be lost at sea, running from a past he couldn't change and in the process destroying the future he craved.

Now, though—thanks to her—he had not one but two fathers waiting in the church for the ceremony to start.

It had taken some time before he'd been ready to reach out to his biological father, but he was glad he had. He liked Niccolò a lot, and Marina had been generous in giving them the space they needed to connect.

So now he felt like the luckiest man alive.

His eyes locked with Giulietta's and he felt his heart turn over.

He was the luckiest man alive.

She was the sexiest, strongest, smartest woman in the world, and together they had made a beautiful, healthy son.

Chest tightening, he glanced down at Charlie. His son was so soft and small he fitted into his arm with room to spare, but his love for him was boundless. As it was for his wife.

'Do you want to take him?'

Juliet turned to Ralph. 'No.' She shook her head. 'He's happy where he is.'

'And you? Are you happy where you are?' he asked softly.

Juliet met his eye. 'I'm happy where *you* are.'

He held out his hand. Smiling, she took it, and they walked into the church together.

* * * * *

Swept away by Italian's Scandalous Marriage Plan*?*
Why not lose yourself in these other
Louise Fuller stories?

Proof of Their One-Night Passion
Craving His Forbidden Innocent
The Terms of the Sicilian's Marriage
The Rules of His Baby Bargain
The Man She Should Have Married

All available now!

WE HOPE YOU ENJOYED
THIS BOOK FROM
H HARLEQUIN
PRESENTS

Escape to exotic locations where passion knows no bounds.

Welcome to the glamorous lives of royals and billionaires, where passion knows no bounds. Be swept into a world of luxury, wealth and exotic locations.

8 NEW BOOKS AVAILABLE EVERY MONTH!

HPHALO2021

#3921 NINE MONTHS TO CLAIM HER
Rebels, Brothers, Billionaires
by Natalie Anderson

CEO Leo revels in his stolen moments with an alluring mystery waitress. Only later, when their paths collide in the boardroom, does Leo discover she's reluctant socialite Rosanna. And carrying his twins!

#3922 THE INNOCENT CARRYING HIS LEGACY
by Jackie Ashenden

Children? Not for illegitimate Sheikh Nazir Al Rasul, whose desert fortress is less intimidating than his barricaded heart. Until surrogate Ivy Dean appears on his royal doorstep...and he finds out that she's pregnant with his heir!

#3923 SECRETS OF CINDERELLA'S AWAKENING
by Sharon Kendrick

Cynical Leonidas knows he should keep his distance from innocent Marnie, yet discovering his Cinderella needs urgent financial help prompts an alternative solution. One with mutual benefits, including exploring her unleashed passion even as it threatens to incinerate his barriers...

#3924 THE GREEK'S HIDDEN VOWS
by Maya Blake

To gain his inheritance, divorce lawyer Christos secretly wed his unflappable assistant, Alexis. Now it's time to travel to Greece and honor their vows...publicly! Yet as they act like the perfect married couple, their concealed chemistry becomes overwhelming...

#3925 THE BILLION-DOLLAR BRIDE HUNT
by Melanie Milburne

Matteo has an unusual request for matchmaker Emmaline: he needs a wife who *isn't* looking for love! But the heat burning between them at his Italian villa makes him wonder if *she's* the bride he wants.

#3926 ONE WILD NIGHT WITH HER ENEMY
Hot Summer Nights with a Billionaire
by Heidi Rice

Executive assistant Cassie has orders to spy on tech tycoon Luke. While he's ultra-arrogant, he's also aggravatingly irresistible. Before Cassie knows it, they're jetting off to his private island—and her first-ever night of passion!

#3927 MY FORBIDDEN ROYAL FLING
by Clare Connelly

As crown princess, I must protect my country...*especially* from infuriatingly sexy tycoons like Santiago del Almodóvar! He wants to build his disreputable casino on my land. And I want to deny our dangerous attraction!

#3928 INVITATION FROM THE VENETIAN BILLIONAIRE
Lost Sons of Argentina
by Lucy King

To persuade the formidable Rico Rossi to reunite with his long-lost brother, PR expert Carla Blake must accept his invitation to Venice. She knows not to let powerful men get too close, but can she ignore their all-consuming attraction?

YOU CAN FIND MORE INFORMATION ON UPCOMING HARLEQUIN TITLES, FREE EXCERPTS AND MORE AT HARLEQUIN.COM.

HPCNMRB0621

*Cynical Leonidas knows he should keep his distance
from innocent Marnie, yet discovering his Cinderella
needs urgent financial help prompts an alternative
solution. One with mutual benefits, including
exploring her unleashed passion even as it threatens
to incinerate his barriers…*

*Read on for a sneak preview of
Sharon Kendrick's next story for Harlequin Presents,*
Secrets of Cinderella's Awakening.

Almost as if he'd read her mind, Leon caught hold of her and turned her around, his hands on either side of her waist. She held her breath because his touch felt *electric*, and he studied her upturned face for what felt like a long time before lowering his head to kiss her.

It was…dynamite.

It was…life-changing.

Marnie swayed in disbelief, her limbs growing instantly boneless. How was it possible for a kiss to feel this *good*? How could *anything* feel this good? At first there was barely any contact between them—just the intoxicating graze of his mouth over hers.

He deepened the kiss and began to stroke one of her breasts. Her nipple was pushing against her baggy T-shirt dress toward the enticing circling of his thumb. Was it that that made her writhe her hips against his with instinctive hunger, causing him to utter something in Greek that sounded almost *despairing*?

The sound broke the spell and she drew back—though in the faint light, all she could see was the hectic glitter of his eyes. "What… what did you just say?"

"I said that you set my blood on fire, *agape mou*. And that I want you very much. But you already know that."

Well, she knew he wanted her, yes. She wasn't actually sure about the blood-on-fire bit because nobody had ever said anything like that to her before. And although she liked it, her instinct was not to believe him, because even if it were true, she knew compliments always came with a price.

Yet what was the *point* of all this if she was just going to pepper the experience with her usual doubts and spoil it? Couldn't she have a holiday from her normal self and shake off all the worries that had been weighing her down for so long? Couldn't she be a different Marnie tonight—one who was seeking nothing but uncomplicated pleasure? She had always been the responsible one. The one who looked out for other people—with one eye on the distance, preparing for the shadows that inevitably hovered there. Wasn't it time to articulate what *she* wanted for a change?

She cleared her throat. "Would you mind speaking in English so I can understand what you're saying?"

She could hear the amusement that deepened his voice.

"Are we planning to do a lot of talking, then, Marnie? Is that what turns you on?"

Something warned her she'd be straying into dangerous territory if she told him she didn't know what turned her on because she'd never given herself the chance to find out. But while she didn't want to lie to him, that didn't mean she couldn't tell a different kind of truth.

"*You* turn me on," she said boldly, and something about the breathless rush of her words made his powerful body tense.

"Oh, do I?" he questioned, tilting her chin with his fingers so that their darkened gazes clashed. "So what are we going to do about that, I wonder."

Don't miss
Secrets of Cinderella's Awakening,
available July 2021 wherever
Harlequin Presents books and ebooks are sold.

Harlequin.com